Letitia had every reason to watch:

Andrew Lockhart—Her beloved, but not altogether faithful, husband, whose pain at her untimely death was matched only by his horror as he gradually became addicted to a strange new kind of love.

Dr. Evan Thomas—A former ardent suitor who now pursued Letitia with an entirely different intent.

Sir William Brookfield—The recently arrived minister of her Britannic Majesty's Embassy, who had discovered in Washington a particularly unhealthy environment.

Beatrice Brookfield—Sir William's nubile daughter, who gave up her admirers for Letitia's deadly kiss.

Bishop Nestor—Sir William's house guest, a kindly, abstracted priest who seemed disturbingly familiar to Letitia.

THE
VIRGIN
AND THE
VAMPIRE

A novel by
Robert J. Myers

A KANGAROO BOOK
PUBLISHED BY POCKET BOOKS NEW YORK

For Tim

THE VIRGIN AND THE VAMPIRE

POCKET BOOK edition published July, 1977

This original POCKET BOOK edition is printed from brand-new
plates made from newly set, clear, easy-to-read type.
POCKET BOOK editions are published by
POCKET BOOKS,
a Simon & Schuster Division of
GULF & WESTERN CORPORATION
1230 Avenue of the Americas,
New York, N.Y. 10020.
Trademarks registered in the United States
and other countries.

ISBN: 0-671-81016-2.

Printed in the U.S.A.

To die! in youth to die!
And Happier in that doom,
    Than to behold the universal tomb,
    Which I
Am thus condemned to weep above in vain.
Why, when all perish, why must I remain?

        —from Byron's poem,
          "Heaven and Earth"

1

The Park Murders

The tone of the evening had been altogether too somber for Letitia Lockhart's taste. There was something about Mondays that produced dull affairs. The idea had been to offer a small dinner for Sir William Brookfield, their neighbor and recently arrived minister of her Britannic majesty's Embassy in Washington, D.C., part of that government's efforts to strengthen relations with the new administration of President McKinley. With Sir William were his nubile daughter Beatrice and their house guest, Bishop Nestor. The Lockharts' immediate neighbor to the west in this park-like section of Georgetown was Dr. Evan Thomas, who had been invited at the last moment when the Welles (Stephen Welles being a colleague of Andrew's in Washington in the Department of State) could not come because of Constance's poor health. She had contracted malaria in Tientsin, China, and the Washington climate had offered no improvement. This had been a disappointment, because Constance was one of Letitia's few close friends among Andrew's associates, the women for the most part being much older than Letitia, at least any that she had met since their marriage last June. Even her relationship with Constance was not what it once was. But without Constance at hand, the conversation had mainly tended toward politics—Andrew was constrained to say the proper things about the McKinley administration, even though he was convinced that in foreign policy it would seize onto every imperialistic venture it could ferret out. This belief had had a depressing effect upon Andrew, and there were rumors about that he might soon resign from the Department of State. What a loss to any government, smiled Letitia. Perhaps it would work, however, to her own gain. Eighteen years roaming about the world was enough for any man, she concluded. It was time Andrew really settled down.

"I'm sorry to see the sun set," said the bright Beatrice. "This is the first time it has shown its face during the past week."

"Rather more like London than one would expect," said Sir William. He had a suitably grave manner, a high balding forehead with tufts of white hair about his long, flat ears. "At least it is not as beastly hot yet as I've been warned."

This was indeed a diplomatic statement, for the perspiration was already trickling down Letitia's back even though she had the coolest seat of all, on top the low serpentine brick wall. Bishop Nestor, however, with his white ecclesiastical collar, and a finely woven and tailored dark gray wool suit, seemed the soul of comfort. "That only confirms, Sir William, the importance of thinking of things spiritual." There was a ripple of postprandial laughter, and the hum of conversation went on, like a swarm of mosquitoes. Letitia, at that thought, shook out her long black waves of hair and rubbed the back of her hand across her cheeks to assure that she was not being quietly bitten by the little monsters. She smiled toward Bishop Nestor, who had a grin on his face most of the time. He was seated immediately to her right on the terrace, the first of a crescent of five chairs leading to the French doors where Andrew anchored that end. The Bishop was an American in language and manner, certainly not English. He volunteered little about himself and was abstract, detached, something not uncommon in the higher reaches of the church, Letitia had noted. Fervor seemed to be the most intense at the lower levels, gradually cooling as it reached the top.

It was really so pleasant on the terrace after dinner. It was during the end of the long period of dusk, the clouds highlighted from the west by the final rays of the dying sun. Dozens of bats darted after the early insects from the park and the neighboring estates in the highest part of Georgetown. Once filled the bats would retreat to the darkness of these wooded acres, including the rambling cemetery. From the front of the house, from Q Street, came the musical clip clop of carriages going to and fro on their missions of social pleasure. They would simply have to entertain more and on a larger scale, Letitia thought, if they expected to carry more weight in political and diplomatic society. Andrew knew that as well as she did, better in fact. She would have to discuss it with him again. Even if he had decided to resign, he would surely want to remain active in society. If he thought she was holding him back in any way, he should say so forthrightly. She didn't think so, certainly, and if there was anything to such a notion, then it was only his priggishness that allowed it to be so. But she shouldn't be cross with Andrew. Not over that.

Certainly they had an adequate staff, more than she really needed. Not counting the Negroes who came in by the day, just for the morning, from the lower reaches of Georgetown's slums, there were already the Negro couple, Amanda the cook and Fowler the butler (elderly, but perfectly capable of turning out a respectable dinner). Letitia was still annoyed that Andrew had insisted on hiring an upstairs maid, an Irish girl Carolyn, dark like herself and no older, to live in. She stayed in the servant quarters in the basement of the main house, whereas the two Negroes lived in the loft over the carriage house. She didn't like having another person in the house at night, in their house, but Andrew felt it was necessary in order to serve breakfast and do the necessary more intimate work in the bedrooms and in his study and observatory. She also helped on other household chores if one of the Negroes was indisposed. He had clearly been spoiled by his Asian tours, expecting to be waited on hand and foot. Letitia was more than willing to do that. She would do anything for Andrew. Carolyn was back in the kitchen with Amanda, while Fowler now appeared with a rattling tray of coffee and liqueurs.

Letitia tried to improve her mood; after all, late May was her favorite time of year. She had dressed prettily for the occasion in a white taffeta dress over a crinoline. There were violet ribbons at the neck and sleeves, and her slippers looked like silver in the twilight. She seemed younger than her twenty-three years, but none of the guests, nor Andrew as well, commented on her appearance. Only Midnight the cat noticed her, rubbing himself against her ankles.

There was a magical quality about the evening—the light mist from the park, the languid smells of the flowers of spring, the pink camellias, the delicate bell-like andromeda, the ubiquitous azaleas (nonetheless as lovely for their profusion), and the pink and white dogwoods running along the garden paths and open places in the park and cemetery, wherever the creative power of the sun could stir their buds. But the flowers of spring only satisfied briefly her sense of completion. What she wanted, right now, was to have Andrew to herself. She loved him more each day, despite their occasional arguments, perhaps because of them. It would be a year, this June 19, when they would celebrate their first wedding anniversary. What would she get for Andrew?

As a matter of fact, she had been shopping the previous Saturday evening. It had been hot, much like this night, and in the cool of the evening, she had started down Q Street west toward Wisconsin Avenue to browse in the shops. Andrew had been to some reception or other—he preferred to go directly from the office, he said, but this did not placate her completely. So it was quite by chance that she accepted Beatrice Brookfield's offer to share her carriage. She liked Beatrice; she was in many ways her opposite, both in her blonde and creamy appearance, and, for example, her dislike of Washington. Letitia had been born and brought up in this quiet southern town, where her late father had taught English literature at Georgetown University, down the hill and closer to the river. Her roots were in Washington. Both her father and mother lay quietly in their eternal rest in the family crypt in the Oak Hill cemetery not far from the Lockhart house. At sentimental times she would visit the site of their mortal remains, sometimes reciting bits of her father's favorite poets, Byron or Shelley, above all Byron. Here too Beatrice seemed to have little interest, despite the fact that they were her countrymen. Her studies ran more to history; she claimed to be reading old English history, displaying in her bag, ostentatiously, Letitia thought, a handsome leather bound copy of Malory's *Le Morte d'Arthur*. They shopped at two antique shops and a jewelry shop— Letitia loved gems; Andrew had given her several star sapphires from his travels in Asia—but they had not really found anything suitable. They did succeed, however, in passing several pleasant hours, and for that Letitia was grateful.

"And do come by soon for tea. Say Tuesday," Beatrice had said.

"I shall be in touch," said Letitia, leaving things at that for the moment. She got off on R Street to enjoy again, by herself, a walk in the growing coolness of the evening.

She could not quite overhear what Andrew was saying to Beatrice, but it sounded as though they were talking about places of mutual experience, perhaps Hong Kong. Poor Andrew, she had first thought, when it seemed inevitable that he would be forced to spend the entire evening talking to Sir William's daughter. Andrew ordinarily did not enjoy the company of girls so young, but Beatrice seemed to be an exception. The two were at the end of the crescent of five chairs. Letitia regretted that she could not readily join them in their conversation. She was envious of the private nods and smiles that passed between the golden Beatrice and the dark Andrew. He was speaking softly and his black eyes, otherwise sad, were luminous and lively and he often showed his sweet smile. For the moment Letitia's eyes concentrated only on Andrew. She felt the skin of her breasts tighten and the nipples become firm against the muslin of her petticoat. His hair was touched with gray, with a slight wave that tousled easily with her touch. His moustache was full and well-trimmed. He stopped by the barber weekly, on Tuesdays, to insure his hirsute neatness. His lower lip was slightly fuller than the straight upper lip, giving him a pouting and sensuous appearance. His cheek bones were small and rather high. His nose was not as sharp as one would have expected from his general thinness, and his brown eyes were set wide apart, conveying a friendly, kind feeling. She never grew tired of watching him, detailing his dress, his mood, his manner, as though he were a natural monument, or a Michelangelo bronze. And it was still the more exciting to know that he was hers. It was because she loved him so much that she could not help admiring everything about him. She approved of his new nicely tailored black frock coat, with the tails ending at the bend of the knee; his trousers were tight and there were secrets to think of in that regard. His white collar was well starched, and from a distance, looked like a clerical band, like that of Bishop Nestor, who was sitting in the chair just to Letitia's right. The Bishop was enjoying an introspective moment, and Letitia was reluctant to attempt opening a conversation with him. Would he ignore her, or dismiss her curtly, or might he probe her intellectual depths and in the end find them too shallow? Yet by doing nothing, everything was happening. She began to understand the wisdom of the Chinese sage Lao Tze that Andrew admired. "Do nothing and all will be done." There was certainly something to that advice from time past.

If she could only believe that—that quiescence was the answer to life's ambitions.

She somehow felt the need to seize the moment. To Letitia, time seemed both transient and endless. She missed the precious and timeless life of the university, the contemplation and the evening sherry. She missed the company of her dead father. She brushed those thoughts aside, however, as she observed the growing animation between Beatrice and Andrew. Should she suggest a rotation of partners as the coffee and brandy were served? It was really up to Andrew, but he was ignoring his duty as host.

That left the matter in her own hands, if anything was to be done. Should she suggest to Evan a stroll about the terrace, or perhaps take him into the drawing room and entertain at the piano with Brahms or Beethoven? She was tempted. Andrew was really being carried away by that vixen. Evan would most likely welcome Letitia's intervention, even though their relationship had become distant. She noticed that he drank his brandy swiftly rather than thoughtfully. He was ordinarily a sturdy, dependable man, sandy haired and tan complected, in his mid-forties, a contemporary of Andrew's. There could be no doubt about it. In some ways he reminded her of her father. Perhaps this was why her feeling now as she observed him—she was growing annoyed with Andrew and could no longer bear to watch—was more a feeling of guilt than anything else. Her intention had been only one of frivolousness, a flirtation, an amusement while Andrew had been traveling to Montreal last fall on Department affairs. She had done it out of a mean spirit. Evan had known her well for some years, when she was a student, and she had loved him desperately. But he made no commitment and she was devastated. For a time she hated him, his dullness, his lack of imagination. Meeting Andrew, however, had provided such a pleasant outcome to her romantic longings that she realized how fortunate she had been that her affair with Evan had been incomplete. And even better, she was certain now that he regretted it, and it was to her own amusement that she toyed with him on occasion for the single purpose of making him suffer. Her success in this regard had been so great that he had made no effort to see her alone since Christmas.

Evan's agitation appeared to arise now in regard to Andrew, toward whose conversation he seemed to bend both eye and ear. Could it really be that Evan himself was interested in Beatrice, and that he was trying to conjure the courage to interrupt that tête-à-tête? Yes, that might be it. Letitia would certainly do all that she could to encourage Evan in Beatrice's regard. She refused to share Andrew with anyone. It might not be out of the question at this moment to announce, "Lady Beatrice, you are carrying things beyond the normal requirement of social intercourse." She could picture Andrew rising to his feet, offering an apology. Perhaps Evan would say, "She hasn't been well, you know. She really isn't herself." She smiled and blushed. She lowered her head, although she knew no one would notice her in the growing dusk. She was probably being over-sensitive, jealous of Andrew's normal, necessary attention to the daughter of the guest of honor. She could not, however, eschew totally her fantasies. If Andrew persisted in his attention to Beatrice, she might resume her game with Evan. Encourage him a bit. Or would he now scorn her? It was silly to become so easily annoyed and to think such thoughts. Above all, she knew, she was terribly bored.

Her sighs joined those of the wind in the oaks. It smelled like rain, coming up from the south, hot and muggy. In the advance were tiny hospitable forks of lightning. It was about time to return the party to the drawing room. She looked toward Andrew again, like a dutiful and jealous wife, which she was. In this half-light, she suddenly noticed that Andrew looked more tormented than before. He seemed tired and older. He had taken on a larger and larger load of worry, especially in the Department of State, where he was expected to perform miracles without the accompanying wand of rank which would have made more things possible. Politics were the rage, but how could anyone not like Andrew? Andrew eased his personal disappointment in the refracted light of his new telescope: in periods of discouragement, he would stay up half the night, his eye and mind on the stars. But all along Letitia was there to comfort him, if he would but turn his mind at those times in her direction. "Tell me, darling, what the trouble is," Letitia would ask of an evening, soothing his brow and fingering his hair. "There is nothing in this world that we cannot solve together." He would in turn squeeze her to him, but as often as not he would keep his own dark thoughts, ideas she knew not what, circulating through his brain, lost in speculation she knew not where.

Andrew had retreated into his own shell: as though however bleak that shelter was, he felt a certain security there. And it was harder and harder to coax him out, as though he were a young deer who, as a fawn, would take clover from one's hand, but each week would become more skittish until no delicacy at all would summon its shadowy presence.

It made her sad that so much of her love was under-utilized. It was too precious to allow it to collect into a great pool and then watch it slowly sink away. Andrew was too preoccupied to wonder about such things. What about Evan? Had he noticed that in unguarded moments, when for no apparent reason, a tear would form in her eye, and as she wiped it away and smiled and her eyes were brighter than ever, she was her most beautiful? After all, Evan was a doctor and was trained to observe the tiniest change in people, of their bodies, their appearance, their attitudes. But she doubted that he had ever noticed anything of that kind. If he did, she hoped it made him suffer again for his lost opportunity. It had all really been his own fault, but then he was no philosopher. He had not really been as helpful as he might have been in the winter when she was so sick with a strange fever. And Evan was reputed to be at the top of his profession. But she preferred to think no more about Evan at all. Was that because she loved Andrew too much, to the exclusion of everyone else, almost any other kind of human relationship? That was silly. And not entirely true, either, even though she would have preferred otherwise. Her own desires and the realities facing her life were contradictory. Perhaps that was why there was the prospect that Andrew did not love her sufficiently. He did not tell her so often enough, and even then, she would have to drag the confession from him, like a medieval torturer, complete with a rack and an Iron Maiden, to show that she was serious. Tonight he had been playing with her, teasing her, as he spent so much earnest time with Beatrice. On the other hand, there were dozens of ways that he demonstrated his love for her in smiles and looks and touches, the tiny attentions that in the end add up to love. She had no real evidence to be uncertain of Andrew, nor he of her. Letitia knew her fantasies grew brighter as the night deepened and the moon and the stars appeared like torches, leaving the still scene bathed in a quiet soothing light. When everyone was gone and Andrew was tired of his astronomical calculations, she would go to him and say, "Now, listen here, Andrew. You have no need to study the stars on my account. They do not govern our future. That is up to you and me." What would he say to that? His interest in astronomy of late seemed almost morbid. He really preferred the telescope to her for some urgent reason, an exasperating state of affairs. His talent lay in history and especially in foreign languages, which he spoke with easy fluency.

She yawned and grew impatient. Aside from Andrew and Beatrice, the conversation was desultory. Evan now seemed lost in thought. Bishop Nestor, between herself and Sir William, nodded pleasantly over his brandy. Being a Presbyterian, it pained Letitia to see a man of the cloth partake of alcohol, much less smoke a pipe. The cut of his ecclesiastical clothes was a shade too rich for her fancy, yet his face was kindly, with crinkles about his soft brown eyes and mottled but not unattractive skin, very tight, almost translucent over his high cheek bones. His thinning brown hair was streaked with gray. There was something familiar about him, yet she did not remember having seen him before. He had been included in the dinner party only because he was Sir William's guest. Evan had even taken to him, a reversal of his usual barely civil treatment of men of religion. Andrew had been proper, but he had made no special effort to draw him into discourse, considering his self-imposed obligation to Beatrice.

There was for no apparent reason a sudden pause in the conversation, similar to the aftermath of some social embarrassment, such as the dropping of an irreplaceable Dresden demitasse cup. In the brief clearing of throats and shuffling of feet on the terrace, it was Sir William who broke the silence. His voice was slightly out of control, alternating between too loud and inaudible, due to deafness that had come along with the years, a certain companion of his golden years.

"I say, Dr. Thomas, was it not close by that that unfortunate young girl was found . . . murdered? I briefly noticed the story in the evening newspaper—the *Star*, is that what you call it—just before coming by."

"Why yes, it was. Scarcely more than a hundred yards away."

"Ghastly business, what, child molestation. The culprit should be drawn and quartered, I say, eh, Bishop?"

"I have no mitigating word for such a criminal. Though a pity, yes, Sir William. To me the soul of even such a one, through remorse and repentance, is still a precious commodity."

"Perhaps on the highest possible spiritual level," said Evan evenly. "I was summoned by the precinct captain to the scene. It has, I confess, cast me into a melancholy that I shall not quickly overcome."

Was that the true source of Evan's general dispiritedness? His behavior of late had been unusual insofar as Letitia had been able to observe it. She had seen him walking about the garden late at night, peering over the wall into the park. Also, he had stood in the very center of the garden, looking up at their bedroom, like a peeping Tom. And just a few nights before, she would have sworn that he had been into their grounds, separated from his property only by bushes, peering here and there, as though he were searching for something. So it was the murder of the child that had come so near to unhinging him. How very strange, she thought.

"Are there any clues?" asked Beatrice. "There was an incompleteness about the account, as though the authorities were withholding information, or were simply at a loss."

"The investigation is still going on. The authorities are concentrating on the park, interviewing people in all the homes bordering it, and turning over every leaf and rock. They are looking for clues that will resolve this ghastly business," said Andrew.

Indeed they were. And not only the constituted authorities. Shortly before the guests had arrived, Andrew had intercepted a bloated, toad-like man claiming to be a detective, a private detective, at the door of the kitchen leading to the alleyway which opened onto the street. All the servants had already been interrogated by the police earlier in the afternoon, and under this kind of stress, there was no way to tell what they might have said, were it not for Andrew's timely intervention. The heavy set, perspiring detective had fled before his imprecations and his threatening walking stick. Despite the intruder's obsequious manner, however, there was a dogged quality to his departure. He had stood under a tree, on the other side of Q Street, blinking at the house for a good ten minutes before he started down the street in the direction of Wisconsin Avenue. Andrew had been furious, yet to hear him now, one would appreciate the control his years in the diplomatic service had wrought. She listened attentively as Evan provided a few details on the location of the body, its placid composure, and the absence of its shoes.

"A substantial reward for leads is being offered by the child's mother, Mrs. Clarence Woodward. Poor soul. She is distraught. It was a completely senseless crime. And besides, she has had more than her share of tragedy recently."

All seemed familiar with Mr. Woodward's death on Capitol Hill the previous week, having been trampled by a runaway carriage after a long lunch with the senior senator from New York. The combination of finance, rich food, and aged whiskey had left the departed financier a single step less agile than was required to avoid the horse's hooves. In his case, however, there had been a general feeling of appropriateness—that he had met the kind of fate that Heaven would decree for the wealthy and foolish. It was his demise that made the death of the child so poignant, pointing up, as it did, the exact converse, that here indeed had gone a tiny bud which now would bloom only in Heaven.

"This sort of thing is not usual here in Georgetown?" asked Sir William, not so much as a question but as a demand for assurance on that point. "I mean, one expects law and order as a matter of course."

"The neighborhood is quite safe," said Andrew. "It's as desirable as when I first bought this house, eighteen years ago. A sensational case of this kind raises everyone's apprehension, but it is unlikely to recur."

"Yet, less than a month ago, there was a similar case," said Evan, "on the other side of the park, near the cemetery."

Letitia felt the evening conversation had taken an unacceptable turn. After all, one should not wish to unsettle the foreign guests. But it was not for her to interrupt the discussion. Once again she relied on Andrew's superb social sense, and this time she was not disappointed.

21

"The breeze has died down," said Andrew. All the guests looked suddenly about as to confirm the truth of his declaration. "I suggest we go inside to avoid any early mosquitoes."

How easily he concealed his concern, thought Letitia, how nicely he smiled at Beatrice. Would his new-found deviousness complicate their increasingly difficult relationship?

There was a general shuffling of the wooden chairs on the stones of the terrace. "Really, Lockhart," said Sir William, "I think it is time for all of us to express our appreciation for this splendid evening."

Andrew accompanied the party through the drawing room.

"Are you coming to the reception at the Embassy Saturday?" Letitia heard Beatrice ask Andrew. She did not hear Andrew's reply. A ball! Would Andrew take her? He would probably scowl and repair to his telescope. Or would he secretly accept Beatrice's offer? Had it come to that? Letitia could not believe so, but at the same time, why had she so easily fallen into this horrible form of self-torture? She absolutely needed more social activity, more companionship. Sometimes she thought Lord Byron was her only true and dependable friend. She often accompanied him in her imagination through the Swiss mountains as he told the tortured tale of *Manfred*. Would she do so again tonight?

Soon sounds came from the street as the guests bade their good nights. It would be comforting to the guests to have such short distances to go, especially in the aftermath of so much talk of robbery and . . . murder. They would be reassured by the gas street lamps as they walked to their respective homes. The thin arc of the waning moon framed Andrew against a mighty oak, visible at the end of the alleyway that led along the house from the back terrace to the street.

Letitia moved from the brick wall to the wicker chair where Beatrice had been sitting. It still smelled of camellias. She could hear Andrew returning. Would he scold and caution her once again? He really was too quick to find fault, question her judgment and her honesty. She knew nothing about that child actually, nothing at all. She sighed again, and with no outsider about, she became visible. Life was terribly difficult for her, and Andrew as well, now that she was a vampire.

2

The Sweet Sad Life
of Chauncey Dawson

The rain adumbrated by the heavy evening clouds had materialized, and the next morning, on Tuesday, there was a wet sheen on the brick streets. Chauncey Dawson moved his great bulk up an alleyway from the edge of the river, along the side of a low warehouse in sorry disrepair, on the Georgetown waterfront, short of Key Bridge. The humidity remained high and all in all this day was of little improvement over the previous one, save that the fiery ball of the sun would not seek out Chauncey and try to melt him. His disappointment and worry at this moment, however, was how to obtain, claim, or capture the $5,000 reward offered for the apprehension of the murderer of the Woodward child.

$5,000 dollars. He could feel the silver dollars trickling through his fingers, each silver stream transporting him away from shame and poverty, into the real world of hotel lobbies and linen napkins on the table.

He had covered the scene of the crime after the police had left, and to his astonishment found one patent leather shoe that must have belonged to the unfortunate child. As he stood at the edge of the park, by the wrought iron fence that divided it from the old cemetery, as though there was no other way to separate the quick from the dead, he held the shoe high in a sense of victory. He would march directly to the Woodward house, where he had been turned out yesterday, his proffered detective services scorned. In good time, however, he realized that his producing the shoe would indicate only one thing to Captain Eric Logan: that Dawson himself was the principal suspect. That's the way that would work; he had traced the likely reaction to the shoe in all directions and that was his conclusion. Their deduction would be completely unfair, but Chauncey knew better than most that justice was a mysterious, uneven process. In his case, he should have long ago been jailed for a particularly juicy piece of embezzlement he had committed in California. Yet justice was on hand again, denying him the sparse but steady comforts of the jail cell and instead, allowing him to remain a free man, living a wretched life on the outer edges of American capitalistic society, being punished at his own expense, forced to use an assumed name (outside his familiar milieu he called himself "Myron McLeod") in case the police were still actively concerned with his crimes.

This society had no place for the unapprehended criminal, which was why earning the Woodward reward was so important. Money would propel him past his shaky status, reclaim his once robust health, and spare him of the everyday humiliations. Lately he had been thinking of nothing but the river, but the single step into its all encompassing flow was a virtue beyond him. Justice required that he carry on. He could picture himself, however, dead, on a marble slab in the morgue, his thin black hair plastered to his large and noble head. "There is no identification," the attendant would say. He could feel himself being slid back into a locker, cooled by ice. His body would soon rot in a pauper's grave in the Georgetown cemetery. He had on occasion walked through that site, brooding over his ignominious plight and suffering over the graves, here and there, sunken by the collapse of the wooden coffins. They would be topped again with earth and leveled, and the grass would grow, and the bones would resume their cramped rest. He shivered. Surely there was a happier ending to his story.

At the top of the hill, at the foot of Wisconsin Avenue, Dawson paused. It was just seven o'clock. The wagons and pedestrians were moving south toward the main part of the city, coming down Wisconsin and up from Reservoir and Foxhall roads. They joined at M Street for the march to Pennsylvania Avenue, the business section, then Capitol Hill. Chauncey's destination was the barber shop on the west side of Wisconsin. It was owned and operated by his Civil War comrade, Gerhardt Schneider, who allowed him to use the address and telephone as his detective business address and paid him fifty cents a day to sweep up the day's cuttings and tidy up the bathtubs and wash basins in the shop. It was the most prestigious barbershop in Georgetown.

Chauncey loathed the job. He considered the work demeaning, but what could he do? He had a past but no future. The happy days, the brief fame he had found was in the detective profession serving the famous Allan Pinkerton during the Civil War. It was Chauncey who had alerted Pinkerton to the plot of southern sympathizers to assassinate President-elect Abraham Lincoln in 1861 when the inaugural train passed through Baltimore on the way to Washington. Chauncey had been but twenty-five and that event stood as the apex of his career. Since then, he had moved with the railways west, working for years for the Union Pacific.

It is the nature of detective work that there is an interface with the criminal world, and it soon becomes apparent that those arrayed against the law have the better of it. And thus Chauncey Dawson had pursued his irregular career, neither being totally honest nor completely crooked. His reward had been the dregs of fear and poverty. He knew that to return to Pittsburgh, where he had relatives who might rally in his time of need, was inviting jail: the authorities would be alert to such a tactic. So he kept to the edge of Washington, literally hidden along the river bank in a dark corner of a crumbling warehouse. Under his hated but necessary name of McLeod, he earned his steady fifty cents a day in the morning, and spent the rest of his time trying to cadge honest detective work, waiting with patience, even resignation, for the grand chance.

"But what is the reason for changing your name, Chauncey?" asked Schneider, when Dawson had appeared last fall and made himself known.

"I'm working on a special case," Chauncey had said, casting his head over his shoulder to be certain that their conversation was their own. "That's why I must take steps to conceal my identity. I expect to crack it soon."

Schneider nodded gravely, unconvinced.

The thirty odd years had not served Chauncey well. All the basic elements of his once rather handsome appearance were gone. His eyes bulged from their sockets; the whites of his eyes had long been tinted with an orange cast; the flesh below was dark and wrinkled in pockets, left there by his dedication to rum. His bowler sat tightly on his balding head as though it had been screwed into place. The jowls puffed out as did the fat on his neck, pushing out over the collar, which was always too tight, and soiled. The texture of his skin was still remarkably smooth along the cheeks. The nose was partly lost in the expanse of cheek, but its redness and the purplish veins safeguarded its identity. Teeth were missing top and bottom, like a piano keyboard. His old black suit, garnered from the discards of Georgetown's finer homes, had served him through the winter, not well, but well enough to keep most of the cold from his vitals; the same suit now added to the heat and discomfort of late spring. The bulk of his shoulders and his belly placed great strain on the seams, and here and there several had lost the unequal contest.

Chauncey was plainly excited, mopping his face at every step as the perspiration flowed. He placed his suit coat over his left arm as he neared the barbershop. The red and white pole turned before him like a stick of children's peppermint candy. The parts in the puzzle of the Woodward child's murder all seemed to whirl before him. He could not slow down the bits and pieces that floated through his mind like the bright color design of a kaleidoscope. His luck would surely turn. With the $5,000, he would escape. He would show them. What made this all seem real and even possible was the fact that he had experienced a remarkable night. Thinking of it once again caused a great palpitation of his heart, and he sat down to rest on the wooden bench in front of the barbershop. He sat as quietly as he could during such moments of stress, hoping that after the wild flutter and the new rivulets of perspiration, he would be all right once again. So far, his theory had been completely borne out by the circumstances. It had been tested to its outer limits the previous night.

The storm had broken around midnight. There had been a rush of wind and the roof of the old warehouse groaned and the tin buckled and snapped. In his corner he had put together the necessities of man's transient existence on this earth—a bed of old blankets and comforters which, made or unmade, had the appearance of a rat's nest; a salvaged Franklin stove, the source of heat during the cold of winter and the source of what warm food found its way into the labyrinth of his stomach. The door he had open to allow for ventilation: he was more afraid of suffocating than he was of an attack by other indigents who in the warm weather often stayed along the river bank, and competed with him for the bounties cast up on the shore from the rise and fall of the tide as gifts from the river.

After a half hour or so, the rain was over, leaving a deceptive feeling of coolness. The humidity was now at a saturation point, and Chauncey in his pool of sweat finally launched his huge belly upright and made his way through the door of his room into the warehouse proper, then out one of the great sagging doors to the edge of the river. There were lights from the barges south toward Alexandria. He sat on a wooden packing case, slapped at an occasional mosquito, and was rewarded with a breeze coming down river from the north and west. There was reason to hope for a clearing spell. Chauncey had not been so careless in his change of scene from the wretched room to the riverside to forget his bottle of rum, and he hungrily poured a quantity of the seering liquid down his ever-eager throat. As he wiped his lips with the back of his left hand, however, he realized that he was not alone. There by the warehouse door was a luminous apparition, a dark woman dressed in white, in a kind of shroud. She stood quietly, then peered into the dark tunnel of the warehouse and disappeared. His fear was replaced by curiosity, and so he quietly moved toward the warehouse, exhibiting the grace of movement often admired in really fat men. He listened at the entrance and hearing nothing, moved silently to the open door of his own room. He could see nothing. He struck a match on the Franklin stove and quickly lighted the kerosene lamp; he concentrated on adjusting the trimmed wick and replaced the mantle. In the farther corner by the bed stood his visitor.

"I apologize for my intrusion," she said sweetly, "but the storm was getting worse."

Chauncey looked at her warily. Part of his wariness, however, came from his poor eyesight. His oversized magnifying glass, the badge of his trade, was his constant companion as he perused discarded newspapers, hunting for leads for his detective business—a spectacular murder which the police would botch, and then for him would come fame and fortune, a great victor's wreath of hundred dollar bills. Truth to tell, however, the only bona fide detective business he had so far come across was from the ribald tales often heard in the barbershop, the horns of the cuckold once again being hung on an unsuspecting husband. Ordinarily the culprit was the husband's best friend, for said friend had the best opportunity to soil his flower. Chauncey had thus quickly turned in evidence on several cases, but had been ill-rewarded. And in the process of importuning a prospective client, he had more than once been asaulted by the wronged husband, loudly declaring that neither his wife nor his best friend would consider such a heretical act. The lumps and bruises of experience, then, combined nicely with the poor eyesight and growing cowardice to freeze Chauncey in his tracks.

"You are most welcome to stay, Madame," replied Chauncey, his irregular smile attesting to his sincerity, "but the storm has now passed, I am happy to report."

She seemed flustered, as though improvising and fabrication were not her usual line of work.

"Actually," she said, with a steady and determined voice, "I've lost something and I thought maybe you had found it."

"I have the misfortune, Madame, to live in these humble surroundings and I do not remember having seen you in my province, so to speak."

"Oh," she said, "it is true that we have not met . . . although I do come around here rather often."

"I shouldn't recommend it, Madame, for I am not certain that a place like this is safe for a lady such as you."

She smiled and advanced toward him. "I have come to help you," she said, and came up closer to Chauncey, who had still not strayed a step from the courage of the lamp. He held his faded, torn cotton wrapper to him, reknotting the cloth belt. But out of his fear and the tightening of his throat, he felt another distant sensation. Somewhat below his massive belly stirred desire.

She was now within his optimum eyesight range, that is, she was in focus, as though his eyes were a camera. She was absolutely lovely. Her wavy black hair fell to the level of her waist and her breasts were barely controlled by the severity of her simple, flowing gown. Her eyes were large and dark, set wide apart above high cheek bones. Her complexion was white, but with a dull pink undertone that prevented her from having a chalk-like appearance. Her lips were pouting and purple red, as though she had been eating grapes.

"I shall come to the point. You have something I want, and if you satisfy that wish, I shall in turn, in good time, see to it that you are rewarded."

Who was this person? Chauncey felt the files and photos stored in his brain, the only system he could afford, flip slowly back and forth, but nothing rose like a long submerged log from the river, to make the identification. Did she really know him, or was this a hoax, a trick of the police?

"You have a shoe I want, a child's shoe."

Chauncey shook his head. His eyes darted wildly and he could feel the dreadful palpitations come upon him. "No, no. I don't know what you are talking about."

"I saw you find the shoe, at dawn, after the night of the murder, when the police had gone from the park."

Chauncey quickly returned to his mental diagram. The Woodward house was on the north end of the park, with only two more estates on that side. To the east side of the park was the cemetery, and then to the south, running along the block from east to west, were a series of homes of diplomats, foreign and domestic, a doctor, a lawyer or two, and a banker. He had covered those houses that afternoon, in his capacity as a private detective, getting little assistance but some idea of the level of agitation. Everything finally had a purpose. To the west was open park, flush to the street. Now if he had been seen at such an hour—and there was no question that he had walked about, trying to develop a theory on what seemed to be a completely senseless crime—the observer would almost certainly have been someone looking from an upper bedroom window, someone perhaps troubled by the tragic event, restless, eyes wandering near the fatal scene and so spying Chauncey.

"I don't know what you're talking about, Madame."

He was terrified as she came an additonal step closer; her eyes seemed to glow, as they left his field of vision, and the smile became a gruesome grimace, the teeth threatening like a wild animal. He instinctively reached toward his throat as he would have sworn she was going to bite him. In that moment, as he released his hold on the upper part of his wrapper, the crucifix of his mother came to his hand, and the apparition stepped back several paces, a look of terror on its face as it flashed briefly through his field of focus. The incident did not, however, slacken her determination to pursue her mission.

"Let me point out the obvious, Mr. Dawson. That shoe is simply your death warrant. If you had handed it over to the police immediately, perhaps they would have appreciated your sense of public duty. And perhaps Mrs. Woodward too. But you did not do that. No. So as things are, the shoe is of no positive value to you. But in my hands, it will prove to be just that."

"I had nothing to do with the murder," Dawson sobbed. "Yes, I'll give you the accursed shoe." Dawson felt the need for rum, but even more, he had to send this apparition on her way . . . even if she rushed directly to the police. He fumbled under the bed. "Here, take it and go."

The figure smiled. "I am as good as my word. The Georgetown police precinct is headed by a man of limited investigative skills. Yet he is required to solve this murder—and perhaps others—or he will be reduced to a mere patrolman. I am a close friend of Mrs. Woodward and I am determined to see justice done. If the murderer escapes it will only be because there are no material clues. Suspicion will be inadequate. But when the culprit is located, I shall arrange to leave this shoe as evidence, and it shall fall to you to report that incontrovertible news to the police and to Mrs. Woodward."

Dawson was weak from fear, and his mind simply would not function. "Who are you? How shall I get in touch?"

"Don't concern yourself with that. Trust me. I shall return—soon."

Dawson stood by the lamp as the apparition vanished. After a few moments, he returned to the bed and fumbled around under it again for the shoe. It was gone. So he had handed it over to her, like a child responding to the arbitrary demands of a parent. He picked up another half-filled quart of rum, which stood by his headboard and wandered out into the night. It was a bit cooler. He raised the bottle again to his lips and felt the fire in his belly rekindle the will to go on, light the hopes of the bright future that too often were extinguished by the emptiness of the bottle. He stood on the low bank and was overtaken by a series of flatulations. He urinated in a steady arc out into the river, and when through, continued to clutch his organ and felt it firm in his grip. He marched on back into the warehouse with his prize and the silent enjoyment of his pit-like room.

Andrew Lockhart was among the early customers in Schneider's barbershop. He planned to go from there to Alexandria, on the other side of the Potomac, to learn whether his chandler had in fact received the shipment from London. He should have placed the order sooner and he regretted his procrastination. He had known all along that there was nothing else to do. Then he would return to the Department and wrestle with the day's problems, disputes and disagreements, real and imagined, with Spain. He had hoped to be appointed as Ambassador to some European country by now, but he had not been able to get a real connection into the inner workings of McKinley's government. He felt more and more like an outsider. He knew too, though he disliked admitting it, that the quality of his work had deteriorated since Letitia had succumbed to the fever last December, then returned in February as an Un-Dead. He was at a loss as to how to handle this delicate matter. He had been distracted and indecisive at the very outset. He had wanted her so much, under any terms and conditions, that his judgment in the end was clouded. Time had run out quickly, and if he could save her at all, it would be a kind of miracle. But he was determined to try.

Andrew lay back in Schneider's barber chair, a hot towel covering his face, save for the tip of his nose. It was so comfortable that he wanted to sleep away the day, but he could ill afford more delay. The argument, no, discussion, with Letitia last night after the guests had gone had at least narrowed the options. And the timetable.

The crux of the matter was that Letitia would simply not take his advice. She would come from her family's crypt in the cemetery each night, in a desire and passion that were beyond human proportions. At first he thought that her nightly forays, her shopping ventures, her appearances on the edge of social events, were a kind of childish petulance, an irritation at being robbed of a longer natural life. But no, he realized that her desire for human society was something beyond her control. This was in itself dangerous, for the wooden stake through her heart would be society's answer. The concurrent aspect of vampirism, the corollary of the blood lust, was the issue that made the whole condition intolerable. It was only a matter of time until she was discovered. She finally realized that, even though she denied killing anyone, ever. All she wanted was to share in their blood.

Under the hot towel, Andrew could again see in his mind's eye his first certain knowledge that the ravages of the strange fever were the temporal evidence that Letitia was undergoing a kind of spiritual rejuvenation. Even then there had been a dreamlike quality about seeing her. But he remembered vividly the first time she had revealed herself to him after her death. She had been dressed in the simple cerements of the grave, more attractive than frightening in her glowing appearance. Her hair was blacker, more silken than ever; her thin, arched eyebrows enhanced her bright black eyes set wide in her thin-boned face. Her smiling lips were sensuous. She had approached Andrew from a mist, or moonbeams, that flooded into his bedchamber, now in his sole possession, like the castle captured by a knight, his triumph saddened by the knowledge that he is the solitary survivor of a bloody assault.

While he could see her perfectly well, he could neither move nor talk, as though he were under the influence or spell of a new and powerful anesthesia.

At the foot of the bed, she had cast aside altogether the garments of the grave and he could smell the overpowering sweetness of gardenias, her favorite flower. She had knelt beside the bed, and slowly began to stroke the glans penis, urging it to life. So intense and real was his dream and so long had been his deprivation that he had been powerless to resist, and in his omission of efforts to force her away, he had watched himself grow in her hand like a blushing rose. He had partially averted his gaze in terror and fascination as she covered his organ with her lovely face. All he could see was the mass of black hair, glowing in the moonlight, then a sting of joy and turbulent release.

But the night was not yet over. She had come again into his arms, with sighs and kisses, repeating his name as though from afar, speaking of love and asking him to join her in eternal bliss. Again she covered his member with her moist and scalding genital, at the same time embracing him and inching up his chest with her wet kisses, stopping at his throat, where she kissed and kissed some more, until he again spent himself. Then, without a word, she had melted away into the moonlight and he had slept into the next day as though drugged. Upon waking, the vividness of the experience—he still thought it might be a dream—caused him to examine himself thoroughly, and there on the pink head of his penis were two tiny red marks, a pattern that was repeated on his throat.

It was this kind of love that had captured his sensuality and his imagination, to the exclusion of everything else. He felt as though he were an opium addict, wasted and hollow until the arrival of the deadly stimulant. Beyond the danger of their guilty secret slipping out into Georgetown and the police precinct forces of law and order, he knew that there was no way to avoid an exchange of a certain amount of blood at the height of their frenzy.

"I can't be the sole source of your nourishment, darling," he said repeatedly.

But Letitia had replied, "I want only you, Andrew, darling. I want you to join me soon, so that we can enjoy each other like this not just for days, but for eternity."

Andrew realized that after Letitia had recovered from the initial horror of her plight, she had adjusted quickly to the virtues of this kind of immortality, To be forever young, to have been preserved at the very height of one's physical attractiveness was a kind of blessing. In time it might outlast her profound sorrow over her loss of contact with society. This could be restored, however, if they could successfully move, by stages, into a situation where no one knew them. This was more difficult for him than for her. He had seen a great deal of the world, and his family was old and well connected. There was almost nothing he wouldn't do for her, to keep her by his side. Of all the women he had known, Letitia was the most special. He smiled, however, within the strictures of the steamy towel, as he recalled the brief pleasure of his flirtation with Beatrice the previous evening which had for a moment lifted his melancholy. But it was Letitia who filled his mind with rapture and responsibility. He had learned long ago not to struggle with the inevitable.

Letitia, for her part, fought against an element of her condition, dreading her occasional confrontations with her Master, an ominous figure who demanded her allegiance and forced himself upon her, despite her protests, when his passion dictated. This was a matter that Letitia preferred not to discuss with

Andrew, the notion that her love for him had been compromised more than once by this creature who appropriated to himself the strange powers of the night. But if Andrew joined her, they could somehow elude him and exist only for each other, in a physical and spiritual harmony, the very perfection of the universe.

"If we go on like this, if we drink each other's blood, at some point I shall most certainly join you, as an Un-Dead," said Andrew. "And with pleasure. But what about the practical aspects of this whole affair—providing you with a new earth box, and one for me as well, a plan of where we must go to survive safely?"

"Yes, Andrew, I understand. We must do so quickly. I am afraid that the earth in which I lie cannot be easily repleted. I will grow weaker unless . . ." She lowered her eyes and Andrew was certain she had faced the harsh reality.

Andrew raised his hand. He knew perfectly well what she meant. As the magic of the earth that was in her coffin (how it was placed there she did not know, could not explain) waned, the blood urge was stronger and Andrew feared the murders in the neighborhood and elsewhere in the city might be associated with this unfortunate condition. Captain Logan had been polite enough yesterday in requesting permission to interview the servants, but Andrew had not been lulled by that. He was in fact surprised that he had not found a summons on the hallway table as he left the house. Perhaps leaving at eight instead of his usual nine had given him an extra day to extricate himself from this dilemma. He would make a poor witness. He hoped that the two boxes had arrived so that he could arrange to have them moved to Georgetown. What would be the best way to accomplish that? Then too there was the sticky business of getting Letitia there safely. The authorities might well be watching, and even though he brought her safely to the earth box under cover of darkness, dawn would surely come and she could be lost.

The whole question of the coffin or earth box and where best to keep it had been a point of disagreement. Letitia had wanted him to move the coffin and its reviving soil into the basement of the house. Andrew had raised practical objections on the odds against such a project not being noticed. Further, as she became more active, it would have even been more dangerous to have her so situated, for on the first flight of suspicion, the police would obtain a warrant and search the house from top to bottom. He had had one stroke of genius in guarding against her discovery, which he did not explain to her, for she might attribute other reasons for it. A month ago he had hired another maid, Carolyn, to attend to the second floor and other light duties about the house. She was not too dissimilar from Letitia in appearance at a reasonable distance, and in her bustling about the house during the day, a casual observer would have noted a dark-haired slight figure. This was an odd kind of protection, but until he could make good his plan for her salvation, it seemed a sound thing to do. Had he known that this new employee had been sent there on the instructions of Captain Logan, Andrew would have been less satisfied with his arrangement. Luckily, he had convinced Letitia to stay in the family crypt. There was something secure about the cemetery that he liked.

There was so much to do, now that the decision to leave had been made. He regretted having to abandon his diplomatic career of eighteen years, but there might be an opportunity in the future to renew it. While there were some certainties in life, there was also a roulette quality about it. Had he received his ambassadorial appointment, he could have had Letitia shipped along with his household effects, and in some foreign land, carved out their new existence. But at best that would only be postponing the problem. He would either have to join her on her own terms, or remain aloof and suffer her loss. At the moment he was still caught in this overwhelming passion. And still Letitia was not completely satisfied. This passion was surely destroying him, but the only antidote was a passion even larger, for someone else, or some cause, some project. He regretted that he could admit to none. Of course it was simple enough in the early hours of the morning when, still satiated with sex, the love marks about his secret places, to blame the situation entirely on the love of Letitia. He could see her in the distance, mocking, taunting, as she joined the faint light of dawn.

Andrew opened his eyes to see her better, and instead caught the glint of the razor, coming out of the glare of an electric lamp bulb.

"Kill me!" he almost shouted, as Mr. Schneider looked at him in a puzzled fashion.

"The usual, Mr. Lockhart?" he asked, lowering the razor.

"Yes," said Andrew. "Lightly on the sideburns."

"Did you rest well?" asked the Bishop, as he sipped his scalding morning coffee.

"Quite well, actually, although I woke up several times with the most vivid dreams."

The Bishop seemed to hesitate to inquire into the specifics, as though he had been through that experience to his own embarrassment. Beatrice, however, went on.

"It was as though someone, dressed in black, had come into the room and looked down upon me in great concern and compassion. I seemed to look at him— for I'm certain the dream was of a man—as though disembodied, as though I was outside my own body, looking dispassionately on the scene. The man advanced and then withdrew, the dark and inky form joining the night. It was eerie and I was frightened. I don't recall ever having had such a dream before."

"The notion of the soul leaving the sleeping body is an ancient belief. I can see no harm in it, except of course no one likes to be frightened."

Beatrice paused. "In talking about it, I think I was really more curious than frightened. The figure was saying something to me, calling my name, but I watched myself lying there, not responding, saying nothing."

"I slept the sleep of the dead," said the Bishop. "I fear that I should be more careful with the brandy. I seldom partake of it."

"Andrew Lockhart was most generous to invite us all. I found him as charming as I did the doctor tedious."

The Bishop's eyes sparkled. "I thought the doctor was most attentive toward you. Even though your time seemed well monopolized."

Beatrice blushed. "I suppose one should be slow to pass judgment."

"I should think so," replied the Bishop. "Your capacity to dream should work to your advantage. In the end, they may reveal to you your real preference."

"That would be nice. It would give me something else to do. I'm off to the dressmaker. Then a friend may be by for tea. If you are here, perhaps you could join us."

"Two is often company."

Beatrice laughed. "The friend is a young lady. An unusual young lady. You would enjoy meeting her."

3

The Missing Hose

Letitia lay in her coffin. It was early Tuesday morning. Bleak and parlous thoughts filled her mind. She was worried about Andrew, both for his own sake and for the danger of his self-appointed mission, to save her in time from the hands of the authorities. Whenever she felt herself approaching a semiconscious state, she struggled against it. She was tired and strayed on the edge of sleep. But there was no way to prevent the dreams that disturbed and oppressed her. There was no way to cry out and end them. Her only salvation was the night. She sought refuge in her memories, and curiously her thoughts turned first to home, to the warm security of her youth when dreams and poems were the reality of her life. She could not remember her mother, since she had died in the act of giving her daughter life. But she could recall her father, with the ease of striking a match, her father with the far off

look, dreaming of poetry he could never write, at last
clutching to himself the works of the peerless poet
Byron, a man who really lived the dreams he surely
dreamed. She pictured once again the tortured Manfred in his solitary tower, he the desecrator of his
lovely kinsman's virtue. Sometimes he would try to
call her up from the shadows, to ask her forgiveness
for his deplorable feat. But for now he would try to
set his mind on another course, to lift his own despair.

> The stars are forth, the moon above the tops
> of the snow-shining mountains—Beautiful!
> I linger yet with Nature, for the Night
> Hath been to me a more familiar face
> Than that of man; and in her starry shade
> Of dim and solitary loveliness,
> I learned the language of another world.
> I do remember me, that in my youth,
> When I was wandering—upon such a night
> I stood within the Coliseum's wall,
> 'Midst the chief relics of almighty Rome'
> The trees which grew along the broken arches
> Waved dark in the blue midnight, and the stars
> Shone through the rents of ruin; from afar
> The watch-dog bayed beyond the Tiber . . . .

Would she at last be able to visit those far off places
which she had long seen in her mind's eye, the romantic places where the poets walked and sang their
verses on the summer air? She knew she should not
think of those things now when danger and torment
were so close to her. She understood what Byron
meant when he said of his memory of Rome: " 'Tis
strange that I recall it at this time; / But I have found
our thoughts take wildest flight, / Even at the moment

when they should array themselves in pensive order."

For the first two months in her coffin she had rested continually, rarely conscious. Now she wondered if her long quiescence had not been due to too little invigorating soil. During that time, there would be an occasional buzzing sound in her ear, indistinct voices trying to communicate with her, then nothing. It was as though she were again in the womb, waiting to be born. It was a time of innocence. And even when she was awakened by the Vampire who had brought her through the veil, she had felt more exhilaration than despair, more excitement than fear, as she began her new life. She had had no occasion to think about the enormity of her situation, the implication of the fate that might befall her as an Un-Dead in still familiar terra. Once an Un-Dead, once again experiencing Andrew and the noctural life, in the manner of a child at Halloween, she began to cherish her condition, which she assumed would be, in a satisfactory way, an eternal existence. There was no longer the worry about growing old, for example. That pleased her. She recognized the wisdom of Benjamin Franklin: everyone wishes to live as long as possible, but no one wishes to grow old. Gross and thin, tall and short, men and women, they all sought the magic of eternal life, not realizing that the Fountain of Youth lay elsewhere, nearby.

It was the intermixture of her new life and old that left her confused, and so often, terribly unhappy. She still knew fear and worry and guilt. Why had they not flown away? She rested poorly. She turned over in her mind some early lines of *Manfred*.

My slumbers—if I slumber—are not sleep,
But a continuation of enduring thought
Which then I can resist not: In my heart

There is a vigil, and these eyes but close
To look within; and yet I live, and bear
The aspect and the form of breathing man.
But Grief should be the Instructor of the wise;
Sorrow is knowledge: They who know the most
Must mourn the deepest o'er the fatal truth,
The tree of Knowledge is not that of Life.

Despite what Byron said—and she did not contest
that he was most likely correct—she longed to know
when she had been fated to become a chosen one, a
vampire. She remembered the time well enough. In
early December, when the white oak in the fireplace
in their bedroom was all but fine ash, out of the glowing coals came two fiery eyes and a pink mist, and the
Vampire, her new Master, was upon her, doing strange
and delicious things to her body. She had awakened,
spent, weak, and deliriously happy. Andrew looked at
her strangely, concerned, and when the fever was upon
her that evening, he sent for Evan. Poor Evan. He too
was mystified. Finally, on Christmas eve, she heard
him pronounce her dead, and the next day, wrapped
in the cerements of the grave, she had been placed in
a simple pine coffin and lowered into a marble vault
in the family crypt in the Oakhill Cemetery in Georgetown. The restoring earth must have been added to her
coffin by her new Master—but only a small amount,
because it had been two months before the power of
the Un-Dead finally rose within her, and she had
hastened to Andrew.

That had been the moment of true awakening, when
she realized that her return from the dead was not the
joyful event of Lazarus at all. It was instead a painful
time, a cause of anguish as well as ecstasy. Would they
ever be able to resolve the contradictions? How she had

anticipated resuming her familiar life, enjoying socializing with real people—friends—and avoiding the dark creatures she now knew lived in the night. Andrew had been remarkably understanding. She had come to him as a petitioner, asking for him to undergo the same rites, but with her in the role of High Priestess. She had explained how the Master looked, describing his frightful appearance, the square, white rectangular face, the black maw of a mouth, the burning red eyes. It was her conceit that, skilfully handled, Andrew could become an Un-Dead without anyone really knowing. She remembered a tale of Lord Byron that pointed the way. Byron's "Fragment of a Novel" set the scene, a man returning to the graveyard of his native village to die. In the completed version of the story, by Byron's sometime companion Polidori, the hero's companion swore a mighty oath not to divulge under any circumstances that the hero was dead. As far as his friends knew, he was simply away. Then he returned as a vampire and was accepted as before, free to ply his new trade.

"The very thing!" Andrew had said at first, but months had now gone by and he still procrastinated. "We must handle this very carefully, darling. What if I were unable to make the arrangements to protect and move you? You would then be defenseless, and surely eliminated."

"The chance is worth taking," Letitia had replied. "I cannot go on like this indefinitely." She referred to her desire to feed only on his blood, although she had realized finally that it was not possible. Not only would he not cooperate, but her needs grew larger daily. She had to wander in the night, like Diana.

Still, Andrew understood her passion. The pleasure of the warm commingling of their blood, their becoming really part of each other, made her believe that he would join her willingly as an Un-Dead. But still Andrew held back; he would not open a vein on his chest to speed the process and make the commitment. He had fears of losing control of his mind, he said; that he would be at the mercy of Letitia's mysterious master, dependent on him for safety and required to do his bidding. Letitia implored him to set aside such dark thoughts and concentrate on her. She too would be rid of the Master, if she could, and with Andrew beside her, in the ranks of the Un-Dead, how much simpler the prospect. She and Andrew together would be serene and complete. They had talked briefly after the dinner.

"Still, I must work out the details of how to move you safely to an environment where we will not again go through this period of apprehension and danger."

"I have not killed a person, I swear," said Letitia, weeping.

"I don't doubt you," Andrew had replied, "but there is murder abroad, and Evan, for one, is very curious. Have you seen him, or more to the point, has he seen you?"

"No," she said, lowering her eyes, "but I have noticed him walking about the grounds at night." Was it possible that he had seen her in the garden, among the spring flowers, waiting for Andrew, and that lost in her own concerns, she had not seen him? His excuse at the dinner for his general abstract and preoccupied condition was the murder, but was this simply an effort to conceal his real anxiety, how to relate such a mind-numbing sight to the previous fact he had known, namely, that Letitia had died and was entombed? Even Andrew had had difficulty facing such an adjustment. And he loved her. Evan didn't. There was the difference and the danger.

"Well, no matter. I am counting these last days. Tomorrow is Tuesday, then Wednesday, then Thursday, then Friday."

"Friday is the day, then?"

"Yes. I will attend to the details and review them with you at the last moment."

She had clung to him tightly, like a child, loving him.

Tuesday wore away slowly. She could not sleep, and there was no resurgence of her strength. She still felt as weak as a kitten. She turned again to Manfred of her memory, and saw his gloomy figure move slowly along the Alpine landscape.

The spirits I have raised abandon me.
The spells which I have studied baffle me,
The remedy I recked of tortured me;
I lean no more on superhuman aid;
It hath no power upon the past, and for
The future, till the past be gulfed in darkness. . . .

She would rely on Andrew. He was a systematic man, exemplified by the way he kept his diary and his astronomical charts. She could never understand the latter, but she could the former. He kept his private thoughts in a clasped leather notebook, secure in her father's walnut desk. She remembered that beloved figure, seated upright in his simple chair, the desk awash with notes and crabby drafts of his monumental study of Byron and his works. However, Letitia preferred the direct access to the poet's mind and the diary would provide the same in regard to Andrew. She had to read it, to know what he really thought.

Perhaps there would be an opportunity during the time remaining.

Her instinct was like Andrew's, that she was under suspicion, that the normal world which both denied and feared the Vampire would not be so easily cheated. It would demand a victim. The question was whether the authorities or, say, Evan, would provide one first, or whether it would be necessary for her to solve their dilemma, allowing for the opportunity for escape. Could she really go through with the plan in regard to the shoe? Yes, in an emergency. Would that crime, a premeditated crime, in no way of passion, weigh so heavily on her already black and burdened conscience that it would in the end suffocate her?

There is a power upon me which withholds
And makes it my fatality to live—
If it be life to wear within myself
This barrenness of Spirit, and to be
My own Soul's sepulchre, for I have ceased
To justify my deeds unto myself—
The last infirmity of evil. . . .

Suddenly there were so many things she really wanted to do, before leaving. She felt as though she were a traveler in some foreign wonderland, who had spent her time rather aimlessly in her chambers, and now as the carriage for the train station was ready to leave the sweeping entrance of the hotel, she suddenly wanted to see the sights, meet more people, have one last talk with her few acquaintances. She would have to hurry or it would all be too late. She thought of Beatrice's invitation to tea. "Say Tuesday." Tea was usually at four, so there was no real possibility for her to go, unless it was a very dark and cloudy day. Perhaps she would go by later.

Finally in the damp and darkness of the crypt, she rested.

"Theories about these murders have jumped about like fleas on a dog," said Captain Logan. "One that has won my fancy is that we are dealing with a basically demented creature, who kills simply for the pleasure it gives him."

Evan Thomas nodded, sucking on his pipe. It was just noon, and he and Logan were enjoying a bourbon and branch water before lunch. They sat in Evan's study, looking out over the rear garden.

"Yes, I quite agree that this is not a normal type of criminal, if one can consider murderers to be a normal part of society."

"And I'm afraid they have been," said Logan, "since Cain and Abel."

"It would be helpful, would it not," said Evan, "if there were a mark placed on the forehead of all such offenders?"

"It would indeed," replied Logan, shifting uneasily in his chair, his left knee pumping up and down, out of control, as though it was an independent entity. The strain marks, the tension of the pressures, professional and political, showed on Logan's thin, shrewd face.

"I have been trying to recall both cases, to see from a medical point of view at least, what were the similarities." Evan had become involved with Logan in the first case by a coincidence. He had been walking in the park when a cry of discovery went up. Evan had rushed to the person's aid and had been among the first to arrive on the scene. As an eminent professor of internal medicine at Georgetown University, his assistance was valued by Logan, and now the second murder had once again brought them together.

"In broad terms, the thing that stands out in my mind is that both victims were ghastly white, and the autopsies both showed that there remained an unusually small amount of blood. The first victim, the middle-aged housekeeper, had a frozen look of terror on her face, while the poor child seemed serene, just as though she were quietly sleeping."

"And of course there is one other similarity. Neither of them had been robbed or molested."

Evan nodded again. "And isn't it also true that both were missing an item of clothing? The belt of the housekeeper's coat, I believe, and in the case of the Woodward child, her shoes?"

"Yes, that is correct."

"As though the murderer wanted to keep a souvenir of the deed?"

"Perhaps. Still, whatever deductions I have so far made, I am at this moment checkmated. Why would anyone wish to do this, and since they are at large, when will they strike again?"

"You don't think there is more than one person?"

"No, that was an error. But when you deal with as many criminals as I do, 'they' often seems to be the proper word."

Evan smiled. "With the political pressure you are under, I can see why you feel oppressed from several directions, why 'they' are on the loose."

Logan shrugged his shoulders in a non-complaining attitude. "Everyone wants results. The problem of motive has of course given rise to superstitious explanations. But in all my twenty-five years in police work, I have never found anyone or anything on the other end of a murder except an ordinary person—such as you or me."

"The puncture marks on the throat are responsible, I should imagine, for that kind of speculation. I have heard the same in the servants' quarters." Evan felt he had let that out a bit too quickly. If he advanced his theory before Logan could be prepared to accept it, he would completely fail to convince him.

"Yes, I imagine. As though it were a bat, or something of that nature. I have simply waved such notions to one side."

"It is true," said Evan, "that in both cases, the victims might have died from fright or shock, that the punctures were not relevant." But the impression Evan left only added weight to what should have been preposterous.

"Let's assume this hypothesis for the moment," said Logan. He lit a thin Virginia cigar and held it in his thin, bony fingers. The crows' feet along his dark eyes deepened as he looked in his bright bird fashion at Evan. "Let's assume we have a demented person on our hands, someone who has fallen so low on the scale of humanity that he no longer operates by our own legal and moral codes. A misfit, a kind of ghoul, would surely be reported. So we must have a situation whereby someone perfectly normal suddenly strikes out, then becomes as before."

"A Jekyl and Hyde notion," said Evan.

"Something like that. Something terrifying."

"Except for your notion of dementia, we are left without a motive."

Logan drank deeply from his glass and helped himself to three fingers of Evan's Virginia Gentleman bottle.

"Of course we might look at it this way," said Evan.

"There was one item of value that was taken—the victim's blood."

"But valuable for what and for whom?" said Logan. "For some strange kind of medical experiment? Is that what you're suggesting?"

Both men were quiet for a time. "I can think of no medical experiment that would require human blood which could not be obtained in less destructive ways," said Evan. "No, I would rule out that notion altogether."

With Logan concentrating on his cigar, Evan raised his bourbon glass. He was drinking too much. He knew he wished to use this frailty as an excuse to blurt out all his worst suspicions. For about a month now, with the onset of warmer and more pleasant weather, he had begun to take evening walks and to gaze at the stars. His interest was purely esthetic, but it was on one of those nights that he had seen the shadows move and a familiar face peer out of a third floor window in the Lockhart house, a face Evan had not expected to see ever again in this world. It was not until the third occasion that he was certain he wasn't losing his mind. Possessing this information was dangerous. Unshared, it led to a private kind of dementia; shared, it might result in social ostracism. He could be abandoned to the special society of the mad.

Evan looked at Logan, who still seemed preoccupied. Logan was under a great strain, there could be no gainsaying that. The pressure was coming from above, perhaps even from the White House. Because of the social prominence of the Woodwards, the murder was the subject of every idle social moment. It had to be solved. Logan was hearing this, day and night, and prodded by the tinges of so many forked tongues, he was restless and alert. And very inventive,

Evan concluded. This was a most dangerous trait for anyone save a novelist.

"Now the question I wish to pose to you again, Doctor, is this: what was the cause of death in the two cases under discussion?"

Evan paused. "As I wrote on the certificates, the immediate cause is not known."

"However, that won't do any longer," said Logan crisply.

Evan's temper flared. "Very well then, Captain, you write on the death certificates whatever you wish. But I won't sign!"

Logan held out his hand, the smoke curling from his cigar. "I didn't mean to offend you. I have here the photos of both of the bodies, and have enlarged the areas of the only noticeable marks, the punctures on the throat."

"Yes," said Evan more coolly, "I noted those wounds at the time. But as you saw—and I thought we had agreed—they did not seem to be a sufficient wound to cause death. Furthermore, there was no blood stain externally and no clot internally."

"Yes, that has continued to bother me, Doctor. Yet we can posit this notion: that the blood was drained out of the victim—either by the suction of an animal, or by a mechanical device."

"An animal? A device?"

"I lean heavily toward a device, a suction pump. A hand suction pump with the motive being only to kill, to terrify, to take pleasure in the awful meaninglessness of the act."

"Any suspects?"

"Perhaps."

"I had hoped that the reason for your suggestion of lunch," said Evan, "was that something more specific was afoot, some angle that you wanted me to follow up."

Logan hesitated. The Doctor was pressing him to get to the point. "One thing," he said, "I should appreciate it if you would keep a sharp eye next door. Anything unusual about the place, any comings and goings . . . out the back."

"Surely you don't suspect Andrew of anything?"

"I have no suspicions, or at least not any I pay much attention to. I believe in piling up facts until they tumble all over the guilty party. I have reason to think there are movements in the night around the place that I should know about."

"I should suggest that you inquire of the new maid."

Logan leaned forward. So the Doctor had guessed she was his informant. Perhaps. "I already have," he said, "but I need corroboration."

"I'll tell you exactly what I see, then, the truth and nothing more."

"That's what I want."

"I wonder," thought Evan, but he said nothing.

"Don't hesitate," Logan reiterated. *"Ye shall know the Truth and the Truth shall make ye free."*

The task of discreetly following Andrew Lockhart to Alexandria proved to be more of a chore than Chauncey Dawson had anticipated. First Chauncey had trouble finding a hansom to take him to the ferry. Then, when he was finally accepted by a driver and had succeeded in pulling himself into the cab, precious moments had passed and Andrew's carriage was out of sight. At last at the ferry, Chauncey had the devil's own time locating the money in his baggy pants to pay off the driver, who sat threateningly in his seat, his whip coiled near to hand, as if to strike. The experience had so flustered Chauncey that he could do little more than stand, sweaty, at the turnstile and watch the boatmen admit the last passenger and lock the ferry's back gate.

Dawson gazed across the Potomac at Alexandria. He could still remember the town as it had been during the Civil War, its docks jammed with supply and hospital ships during the great Peninsula campaign of 1862, in the spring. He had been in Pinkerton's service, attached to General McClellan's staff. After the war, it was written that Pinkerton's information was favorable to the Confederates because it grossly exaggerated the number of troops the Rebels had available for the defense of Richmond. Caution was the most tangible inheritance that Dawson had received from his experience with Pinkerton in the military intelligence business—caution and the reluctance to accept defeat. Gen. McClellan, Pinkerton and his staff had all been removed from the Union army by the fall of the same year, shortly after the Battle of Antietam.

The service with Pinkerton was enough to land him a job as a railway detective. The work was generally tedious and boring and the stakes low. *This* was the kind of job Chauncey was created for. And in his one really serious effort to emerge from the mass of humanity, to strike for the large financial reward, the success had been short-lived. Knowing intimately the workings of the railway, he had uncoupled a boxcar filled with sewing machines which his colleagues were to offload in the dead of night and sell in California at a handsome profit, their cost of acquisition being so low. Instead, the police arrived and Chauncey barely made good his escape, riding the rods. For his imagination and pain, he was now a wanted man, for no greater crime than ineptness.

But there the ferry went without him. He had spent twenty cents for the ride and his quarry had escaped. Perhaps he should station himself outside Lockhart's home during the evening, to keep an eye on him and the dark lady. What were they really up to?

For some time Chauncey stood at the fence of the ferry boat station, puzzling over the situation. The vapors of rum still rose heavily about him, and he could feel the disdain of the pious as they walked primly past him, their own imbibing countered by the eggs and bacon and baking powder biscuits of a proper breakfast. He had thought long about his visitor, her languor and her unusual appearance. And her knowledge of the child's murder and her interest in the shoe. As he had tilted his rum bottle at the highest angle at the conclusion of last night's private party, he had begun to develop a hypothesis. All it needed to take shape was another bottle of rum. In this he was most fortunate. There was a mighty supply close at hand, available to one who had worked the detective trade long enough. In the next warehouse was a bonding room for Puerto Rican rum. It was the work of a few moments to pick the lock leading into the high-ceilinged room. It was a skill of another order, however, to cope with the situation one found there. The one-hundred-gallon casks of rum were protected by iron grillwork, not unlike a jail cell. With great patience and cunning, Chauncey had worked days and nights on end to cut through a section large enough to admit his body, cutting it perfectly, so that it could be fitted in and out easily and undetected to the human eye or the casual thumping of an inspector.

Then came his most successful stunt so far. The barrels were stacked three high. He had succeeded in reaching the top of a second level keg, the second keg in, and drilled a tiny hole in the top of the barrel. Into this he had inserted a rubber hose with a valve, a valve that opened when he applied suction, and into his quart bottle would come a refill. He would then place a cork in the hole on the top of the barrel and no one was the wiser. He was determined that it would remain that way. He knew if he just once appeared in Georgetown or anywhere in Washington selling quarts of rum, it would be all over for him in one day. He did dream on occasion about the possibility of siphoning out one barrel after another and placing it all on a barge and floating it out to sea, where a fair exchange of rum for money could be consummated. But such a scheme would require collaborators and was therefore inherently risky, as he had learned in California. It suited him more and was a great comfort to know that for some years to come he was guaranteed a steady and free supply of good Puerto Rican rum.

The rum worked on him, he felt, like an incandescent lamp, making everything clear, lighting all those dark places of uncertainty and fear. Just as the rum in the early dawn had allowed him to connect the visitor to Andrew Lockhart. The previous afternoon when he had stopped by the Lockhart home to chat with the servants, he had seen someone in the back of the house dark and slight, like the visitor, but before he had an opportunity to talk to her, the man of the house had appeared and with foul and abusive language, driven him out into the street. Now why such a strong reaction to his peaceful inquiry unless there was something right there that Lockhart felt would be endangered if exposed to Chauncey's scrutiny? What other reason could be advanced? Plainly, Lockhart was a worried man. What would worry him more than a murderer on the premises?

Now it was Chauncey's belief, based on his observations of life, that if Lockhart was in such a mood, it was either to protect this mystery woman, a maid already being victimized by the aristocrat, or to protect himself. They knew he had the shoe; he had lumped Andrew and the visitor into one at that moment, seeing their interest in shoes as a common denominator. What had the visitor said? "I shall leave this shoe as evidence, and it shall fall to you to report. . . ." There was something Biblical about this, as though an angel of the Lord had come by with an inspired message. But in the incandescent light now burning in his brain, it was evident that they were going to give someone a bum rap to save themselves. Now one could not depend totally on noctural promises by people who all but floated in and out of his presence, and, he had almost forgotten, fled from the sight of the crucifix. That had been an extraordinary moment indeed, when the visitor had actually recoiled as though struck by a powerful psychic force. As the great light began to go out inside, as the door of unconsciousness creaked on its hinge, Chauncey had determined to learn more about Lockhart and his deeds, about the dark woman in the house, to see if the evidence of the shoe might not be advanced sooner rather than later. After all, the case could now be neatly made and who is to say that the guilty finger would not point in the proper direction.

Finally, Chauncey turned from the ferry station and began the long walk back to Wisconsin and M. He invested no more money in transportation. Instead, he made his way slowly, stopping from time to time to sit under a tree, devour a loaf of bread from a passing vendor, and partake of a handful of early green apples from the edges of the first mountain ridges into Virginia. This had been as unwise as it had been delicious.

He began to feel ill. Perhaps he would be restored by an afternoon nap and a mouthful of rum. He did not want to drink too much more now for he would have to make up his mind about the child's shoe and the police. The walk down the alleyway along the warehouse was easier than going up, yet there was the worry of slipping on the wet bricks and tumbling on down to the edge of the river, a nasty tumble indeed. Out in front of the warehouse, lying on the damp bank and eyeing the cloud-shrouded sun were two derelicts, fishing. Chauncey ambled over.

"Catching anything?" he asked.

"Nothing yet," said one fisherman, his multi-patched overalls clean to the eye.

"What are you using for bait?"

"Worms. Crawlers."

"Good luck," Chauncey said and walked on. He crossed the cinder ash road that separated the warehouse from the river and entered the cool damp of the main part of the building. He turned right, and undid the padlock of his own room. To his knowledge this was the first fisherman on this river who was not fishing for carp and using dough for bait. So he was being followed—by the police? And if so, for what reason? That was the joy of having a questionable past.

He eased himself onto his bed and reached for the familiar bottle near the headboard. He raised it to his lips. Empty. He cursed softly under his breath, and walked over to the far wall, beside the old photo of Lincoln, to take his rubber hose off the wall to repeat the miracle of the never empty rum bottle. But the hose wasn't there. Where was it?

4

Andrew's Diary

It was just eleven o'clock Tuesday morning, and Andrew was pleased that his transaction in Alexandria had gone so smoothly. Hooker, the chandler, had the bland face and easy manner that comes to those who succeed in accepting the extraordinary as the ordinary, for a price. Both earth boxes were in good order, and Hooker had agreed to send them by barge to the east bank of the Potomac at Key Bridge on Wednesday afternoon. Then, early on the next day, he would send a wagon to Andrew's Georgetown address, take some additional items to the barge, and then Andrew would accept the responsibility. The wagon was to come by no later than eight in the morning, a time when Andrew calculated there would be little curiosity along the street. That part of the affair was to his satisfaction.

The matter of leaving Washington, at this juncture,

still rankled. His personal life was wrecking his career. There was the consolation that he might return later, if the departure were smooth enough, but that was so far off. Certainly he was finished forever if the police discovered Letitia to be a vampire, and that he had sheltered her and aided her all this time. But undiscovered so far, he was pleased with himself. He would compare himself favorably to any man in terms of cleverness. And he was wise enough to know that when this feeling was upon him, that was the moment for caution and care to avoid that·one fatal overreach.

The matter of the murders made the decision to move all the more urgent. It was devoutly to be wished that they would be solved, to his satisfaction, before leaving. Otherwise, their sojourn in New York might be unpleasant. Suppose the police were to come by and ask questions and search the premises? He had explained to Letitia that he would take her away, safely, to New York, then elsewhere. This would have to be done skilfully, and in stages. In New York, he had already leased a modest brownstone, where he could place Letitia safely in the cellar; it would be an area where she could find sustenance easily, and the pressure on him to join her in these escapades, as well as the excessive sucking of each other's life-giving blood, would perhaps be minimized. Or if it were not, after a time, they could go on to the second step, to a location, perhaps Chicago, where neither of them were known and they could make a start at the idyllic life that Letitia envisioned.

Letitia. How he loved her, yet rued her! The trouble was she knew it. She needed him (there was no doubt about that) and he could not abandon her because of this accident of nature. He had worn the mourning band in a sincere sense of tribute, but it was difficult for him to settle down, permanently, with a vampire for a wife.

If one were simply content to be a vampire, then that would be one thing; the pleasures of which she spoke were real. But he needed more than the prospect of endless lust and satiation. He preferred the taste of power. He enjoyed pursuing the affairs of the world and of the nation, and the creature in the coffin, his beloved wife, was pulling him away. He had given his word and he would do it. Further, he was determined to enjoy it.

His large office in the Department of State looked out across the way to the west side of the White House. The Secretary, Mr. W. R. Day, was there discussing Cuban policy with President McKinley. There was popular outcry to go to the aid of the oppressed Cubans against the Spanish tyrants. So far McKinley had kept a cool head on the matter, but Andrew was certain, in the end, the yellow press would have its way, either this year, 1897, or the next. His own private secretary, Mrs. Winslow, was typing administrative reports, and there being nothing pressing, he set about writing his letter of resignation, "for personal reasons." The sad thing was that he feared he would not be too much missed. There were small armies of office seekers always in Washington, which was a kind of encampment for hangers-on of all sorts. His own position was more or less secure because of his mastery of arcane languages. This skill or specialty, however, had probably worked to his career disadvantage. He was certain that Secretary Day regarded him as something of an oddity and for that reason not in line for an ambassadorial post, especially having no political connection with the administration. Andrew thought that if Ambassador John Hay, now in England, would return as

Secretary, his own chances might rise again. Hay's reputation was waxing. Sir William Brookfield had spoken in flattering terms, in fact, about Mr. Hay's performance at the Court of St. James. But all of this was idle thinking. Andrew's mind was made up. Above all there were these murders, and certainly more to follow. He would draft the letter of resignation without delay. Time was short.

Although it was only two o'clock, Letitia was up in Andrew's bedroom. She had slept fitfully only until noon. The day was overcast and dark, dark enough to awaken her from her sleep and allow her to rise from the coffin. At the filigreed iron gate of the crypt she paused to look about the cemetery. She looked up and down the rows of markers, her view blocked here and there by the shrubs and bushes and evergreens that grew luxuriantly in the early spring. At length she opened the lock from the inside—coming from the outside, one needed a key, unless they had the good fortune to have the qualities of a vampire. Once outside, however, she was worried. She doubted if she could perform such routine miracles unless the sun were below the horizon. She could not, in short, return to her earth box until sunset. But she would deal with those problems as they arose. She would move across the park, discreetly, and enter from the rear garden gate, then make her way through the garden and upstairs with the stealth of a tiger. She smiled to herself, safely inside the bedroom, the door locked against intrusion. Andrew had not allowed the room to be changed in any significant way; her books of poetry in their leather and gold bindings were still in the familiar shelves along the side of the library. Their wedding photo was on the desk. And knickknacks. She loved to collect odd souvenirs. There were two pillows on the brass bed, despite their infrequent use. Or was there a secret he had not shared with her? Beatrice was so near at hand. She was presumably cloistered, but with the social schedule of her father, she would find occasion to be home by herself, without a doubt. And she did not hesitate to go out alone shopping, for example. She was a dear girl. Letitia doubted that Beatrice would refuse an advance from Andrew, but would Andrew make such an offer? Letitia could see them wrapped together in the dim light, and despite herself, she smiled.

She sat down at her late father's desk and manipulated the extention of the middle drawer until it was just so, then she easily slid open the drawer where Andrew kept both his diary and his notebooks of astronomical calculations. It was not a question of a lack of faith in Andrew's faithfulness, really, but as they came down to their final days in this house, there were things that she wanted to learn or confirm. What was he thinking about, concerned about, on the edge of their departure? For instance, last night, he expressed great agitation about solving the mystery of the murders. "I hope that the police seize the culprit soon, before we go, so that our disappearance is not taken by society and the authorities as evidence that somehow we were involved with these heinous crimes."

"I have sworn that I am not responsible, darling, and I resent that you do not take my word for it."

"I have not suggested that, Letitia, yet you would agree that the deaths seem to be the work of a vampire."

"Do you think that I am the only vampire in this city? Are we not aware of at least the one who took me through the veil, helter skelter? Does not the infection exist and spread? Beyond that, the police will be reluctant to follow fantasy. People in general may believe in vampires, but not the police. Some person, some ordinary person, will be held responsible for the crimes."

"Perhaps so," said Andrew. "Nonetheless, I would like to see the matter quickly resolved."

"I think you should have more confidence in me, darling," said Letitia. After all, she had the shoe, the shoe that in its own way had the lure of Cinderella's slipper. She kept that information to herself and found strength in that power. Whomever the police insisted it fit would be in the limelight.

Now Letitia rose to place her ear to the door. There was no sign of the new maid Carolyn. She turned again and looked over the room carefully. There was now only one rocking chair before the fireplace, and the colorful and fancy headrests were no longer there. Her small collection of romantic novels had been removed. The great cedar chest still guarded the double windows looking out toward Sir William's house. Was Beatrice's bedroom directly across? No, it was in the back, with a nice veranda, from which one could see both the park and the rear of the cemetery. There were no fresh gardenias in the room, even though it was very much the season. She wept.

She sat down in the chair at the desk. There was the possibility of disappointment in opening his journal. It was a little like entering the Garden of Eden. There was the major question of how Andrew accepted the fact that she was a vampire. She was worried. He had behaved impeccably, and had made her feel at ease. But was it real? Had no real sense of shock and horror crossed his broad and tender brow, no wringing of the heart and hands at the discovery? She had to know how he really felt about her. Did he think of her as his lover or as a loathsome creature that he would sooner squash than hold? Was he giving up his life here for her out of a sense of passion or out of a sense of duty? She trembled with curiosity as she opened his private journal. Would he be furious with her if he found out? If she told him?

The first date she checked was the date of her death, December 24. There was nothing, the first subsequent entry being that of the New Year, January 1, 1897. It was written with precision and style. He had copied out a few stanzas of a Byron poem that had become her favorite as the gloom of her mysterious fever clouded over the bedroom, and all could tell that she would soon unwind her mortal coil.

And thou art dead, as young and fair
    As aught of mortal birth;
And form as soft, and charms so rare,
    Too soon returned to Earth!
Though Earth received them in her bed
And o'er the spot the crowd may tread
    In carelessness or mirth,
There is an eye which could not brook
A moment on that grave to look. . . .

The flower is ripen'd bloom unmatch'd
    Must fall the earliest prey;
Though by no hand untimely snatch'd
    The leaves must drop away;
And yet it were a greater grief
To watch it withering, leaf by leaf,
    Than see it pluck'd today;
Since earthly eye but it can bear
To trace the change to foul from fair.

There were many days thereafter in the journal quite blank. Letitia assumed that the sensation of grief had so numbed his mind that he had had no courage to face the fact of her death, no will to drive him onward in the cold and darkness of January.

Then there was an entry on February 24. "A most singular event happened on this night, that even now, in the brightness of the following morning, I am at a loss to explain. But I shall try, for I believe that something unusual—no, miraculous—is happening." He then described the night when she had returned to him. "She knelt beside the bed, and slowly began to stroke the glans penis, urging it to life. So intense and real was my dream and so long was my deprivation, that I was powerless to resist, and actually in my omission of efforts to force her away, watched myself grow in her hand like a blushing rose." She smiled and blushed. So he did love her. He had enjoyed the night as she had. She read on.

At first, Andrew had been of the notion that he had experienced a particularly vivid dream, until he had discovered the two tiny red marks both on his penis and on his throat. He had concluded, "I could not wait to find out for certain what had happened to Letitia. I could no longer take shelter in the maxim that what is not known cannot hurt. But no more for now. My brain is so overcome that it can no longer guide my pen."

The next entry was a week later. She reread the February 24 account, however, savoring it immensely. The magic of their love had indeed not died. He had loved her, responded to her. The turning of the heavy paper made a scratching sound, and she was startled. She turned the page back slowly and then turned it again as she had done before. All was well. The entry was March 2.

"A week passed before my courage rose to match my passion." Letitia was pleased with that sentence. To have really just begun their married life together, the blending of feelings and attitudes that had made their marriage complete, the tensions and their resolution—that was the true tragedy of her temporal death. Some way it had to be reconstructed, in one world or the other. "She (or the dream) had not returned to our bed chamber. I decided that I could no longer leave unsatisfied my curiosity (should I say hope?) that Letitia had indeed undergone this transformation, that I could still see her, talk to her. It was early afternoon. The air was damp and heavy and a wet, thick snow was falling. The cook Amanda and her husband Fowler were in the carriage house, and the evening stew was simmering over the log fire in the carriage house kitchen.

"Roland, our spaniel, went along the one hundred yards or so to the edge of the cemetery. I launched myself over the low stone wall at the edge of the property next-door, east, in a kind of swinging pivot, and Roland bounced along behind me. The Ellicott family crypt is on down the fast descending hill. It is in the center of a natural glade. There is a row of low pines on either side of the path, providing a natural and decorous approach, while the tall tulip trees, oaks and spruce point the way to Heaven. There is a lock on the cast iron filigreed door of the vault. It yielded to my key and creaked in protest of its lack of use. I was in no hurry to smooth the passage of the next most likely guest of honor. There were tapers in the metal holders along the entry way, as well as in the vault proper. As I lit the taper by Letitia's vault, I disturbed the rest of a great bat, which noiselessly followed the path of air and light that came from the open gate. Sheltered by the trees and the natural low setting in the glade, there was indeed a silence associated with the grave.

"The marble lid to the vault was heavy and I struggled to pry up one end and balance it along the top of the vault so it would not fall and break. It would allow sufficient room and freedom for my purpose. At last I had succeeded in my work. The edge of the vault was about chest high, so now I could reach down into it, where the pine coffin lay. The iron pry bar I had in my hands—I was so excited and apprehensive that it seemed as light as a stick—would do its duty and I would see what had to be seen. I was astounded, however, that the lid was loose. The nail holes were clearly there, but the nails themselves were gone. The question was had someone divined my purpose and already taken the body so that there would be no clue to my suspicion? I noticed too, in the interstices between the vaul and the coffin an amount of dirt. It was not the common red clay typical of this area, but rather a dry dirt, with more of a fungus base, a leaf mold. In any case, it had been added after the entombment.

"I paused again before proceeding, dropping the iron bar at my feet, and placing my hand on the lid of my beloved's coffin. There was not a sound; Roland lay outside in the snow, waiting for my return. Finally, my nerves strained almost beyond endurance, I began tilting back the lid. I slipped it over the side, between the vault and the coffin. The light of the taper cast shadows inside the vault, and finally reached down into the coffin itself. It was Letitia, beyond doubt. Instead of the smell and evidence of the natural process of decomposition, delayed so far by the coldness of the weather, she had a new degree of radiance, as though an inner warmth improved her features and her color. In a word, it was as though she were alive. I touched her right wrist, folded in the attitude of death; it was cold to the touch and there was no sign of a pulse. I examined her dear face in detail. Her eyes were closed, and I did not have the courage to open them. It was the lips, however, that provided the ghastly evidence.

"First of all, they were of an unnatural redness, a purplish color as I had remembered. There were also in the corners of the mouth tiny clots of blood, congealed in the cold in balls, some of which had fallen onto her grave garments. Gingerly I worked open her upper lip, exposing her teeth, and not only her canine teeth but the incisors as well, had a more pointed look, the better to fulfill the function dictated by fate. At that instant, Roland howled to the Heavens, the howl then being replaced by a snarl. I made no attempt to replace the marble vault lid. I extinguished the taper, and made my way quickly to the door of the crypt. I could not see Roland, but he was not far away. I walked back into the half light of the snowfall, numb of senses, fearing that whatever I tried to do to escape would be futile. I walked unsteadily to Roland, to grab his collar and head for the house. Like the dog, I was transfixed by the black figure standing in the snow in the middle of the glade. Was it the dark stranger once described by Letitia, the figure of the night who had transported her from our world to his? He was dressed entirely in black, including a wide brimmed hat. His cloak was pulled about him, and his long hands were exposed, the nails extending like the claws of a bird. From the shadow of the brim of his hat, the red eyes glowed, and the whiteness of his teeth contrasted with the dark hollow square of his mouth, which seemed to hiss and laugh, in a horrid way, and from which came the overwhelming fetid smell of the blood-satiated vampire. He had before him on the ground a large brown burlap bag, and from it came tiny cries, almost undistinguishable, but nonetheless unquestionably human.

"Roland responded to my touch and licked my hand lovingly, his rough tongue reestablishing our bond one to the other and restoring a sense of humanity. I stood for a moment, looking at the bird-like presence of the Vampire who had stolen Letitia from me. He appeared as a kind of crane, a black crane, fallen from the heavens, making known its complaint to earth. I slowly started to move away, toward the path leading from the crypt, when the Vampire raised one long and powerful arm, the finger nails protruding like daggers, and in a kind of fearful benediction, caused me to stop in my tracks.

" 'I have come,' said the Vampire, 'not to frighten you or cause you trepidation—that prospect is always and forever open to me—but rather to tell you of your responsibilities.'

"I nodded my solemn acknowledgement, not in terms of approval or acquiescence, but simply the cognizance that I would hear more, the choice having been denied me.

" 'You have witnessed once again my power, the power of overcoming death, the ultimate power sought by the human race. Your Letitia is not dead. She still lives, and you have been the beneficiary of her continuing charm.'

" 'She is saved at a price she would not willingly pay.'

" 'The conceit of mankind is to have eternal life. I have found the answer.'

" 'No one, I believe, would accept such a gift—if

gift it is—under such conditions. It comes from the Antichrist.'

" 'There are philosophers and religious mystics, and there are practitioners. I hold myself high in the application of eternity. Now, you have for some time found the argument for immortality irresistible, having accepted your wife once again as your wife, and all the implications thereof. You must receive her when she wishes. Otherwise, she languishes in her tomb, and if she has no nourishment, will soon pass into the nether regions, beyond your ability to add or subtract. Her likely alternative is to select another lover.' "

Letitia pushed the diary aside. She cupped her head in her hands and stared blankly out into the street. She understood quickly enough the impossibility of her early demand, when she was freshly risen and the terrible appetite was not yet so overpowering. No one person could support the needs of a vampire. The lust for blood grew stronger each day and more and more victims of this peculiar thirst were required. Someday it might subside to more manageable levels. She didn't know. Yet she had been punctilious about her promiscuousness, and in that very fact had found claim and allegiance to her deep love for Andrew. Even now the thirst was sweeping along her throat and mouth. The wall clock said 3:30. Still no alien sounds from the lower floors or from along the carpeted hall of this floor. No padding about of Roland, who had long since been lost—or stolen away—during an unaccompanied walk. Midnight the cat was about, she was certain, probably napping from the usual activities of the night. Life was suddenly a terrible burden, as she realized again the mixed nature of her immortality, how her return had strained Andrew's psyche and his natural consideration into a kind of nightmare of the unnatural.

How she admired his strength and courage. She resumed reading.

" 'Do you say that she will have no one else?'

" 'That is her present position. The choice in any case is hers, for there is no absolute shortage of supply. . . .' As in macabre emphasis, there was again a stirring in the great gunnysack.

" 'I do not believe she would perpetuate herself, be a member of your cult, or whatever you may call it, if her mind were free and her decisions were her own.'

" 'I bear witness to thousands of individual decisions, over as many years,' said the Vampire, his long arms describing half circles and his black cloak rising against the snow, until his red lips and black mouth in the center took on the aspect of a spider's maw.

" 'Have you not once thought of the glory of Heaven, that your foul practice is the single barrier between you and your slaves and genuine life in the eternal Heavens?'

"The Vampire again waved his arms in wide agitated circles. 'What evidence do you have for such a statement? Why do you not instantly recognize the truth of what I am and what I can do before your eyes as the fulfillment of every prophecy? Remember that the Undead cannot forever stay in the same place, because of two practical matters, nourishment and persecution. When I leave, I shall take Letitia with me.'

" 'Release her! Give her back to me.'

"Then without a further word, the Vampire seized up his sack, turned and fled across the floor of the glade, disappearing into the pines and falling snow. Roland raced after him for a short moment, then sniffed in confusion. The smell of the Vampire hung over the windless glen. The dog ran in circles around the place where the vampire had stood. There were no tracks in the snow.

"I realized finally that I would have to make a choice fairly soon, either to allow Letitia to complete my conversion to the Un-Dead through the promise of everlasting passion, aglow like the fires of Hell, or to flee for my sweet Christian life. If I chose the former, I would roam the night, searching for victims. If I departed, I should never see Letitia again and I could not bear that. Either way, however, I would be obligated to remove her from the orbit of this monster. He might at any time decide to take her from me altogether."

Letitia shuddered. So Andrew had known the time dimension of the dilemma from the beginning but he did not flinch. Like Andrew, she too feared the Master. Each glow in the dark she suspected was his evil eye; each flight of a bat might be his transmogrified image. The sound of a running dog and the sight of its drooling tongue reminded her of the Master's other incarnation. She instinctively knew of these powers of the vampire, powers that she feared so much she was reluctant to use them. She preferred to pass lightly among the moonbeams, for as a bat or wolf, she risked being overwhelmed by rival occult forces of the night, risked ever again seeing and loving her lover.

Now she accepted Andrew's hesitancy to join her, his real concern for her. She went on in the diary to the most recent entry, Monday, the night of the dinner party for Sir William. First there were astrological and meteorological entries, the juxtaposition of several planets, and the course of the Sun in its orbit. Then the prospect of improving weather over the next few days. "Friday then is the day of decision. I have tried to postpone things too long as it is. I believe I have the precise date. It is after all the question of setting aside the lesser issues and facing the larger ones. I simply cannot do everything. I cannot fulfill every obligation, every expectation. No, I shall follow love, and in so doing there will be a new beginning. Letitia is in great peril. I shall save her, at whatever cost!"

Andrew, then, would surely take care of this pressing matter. In fact, he must have a surprise for her, a plan to resolve all their problems. *"I shall follow love, and in so doing, there will be a new beginning."*

Letitia went to the west side of the bedroom and looked out cautiously from behind the curtain. Evan was on the stoop of his house, looking up and down the street. He scowled from time to time at the Lockhart house, as though he saw in it something disagreeable. Letitia was convinced that he bore a grudge against Andrew for his success with her, which only illuminated Evan's failure. Evan had a certain courtliness about him, a slowness in expression and style that had handicapped his courtship with Letitia. She much preferred Andrew's hot-blooded, dashing style. She was amused at Evan's interest in Beatrice Brookfield, which she had noticed not only at the dinner but during the previous two weeks when Andrew had called at Sir William's for tea. Beatrice, she felt, was in a mind for proper, or perhaps improper advances, something that Andrew also recognized, but which the plodding Evan didn't. But Evan's concentration on the Lockhart house and not on Beatrice had long forebodings that worried Letitia. Did he suspect her situation? Did he suspect her of murdering the Woodward child? She had sucked her blood, it was true, but she had left the little girl on the ground still conscious. She had not killed her. Letitia was certain no one had seen her during the few minutes after she had coaxed the innocent into the park. She had hovered, invisible, while the police searched the scene and almost at dawn she had observed the fat man's moment of triumph in finding the shoe. She had the other one, all along, but she could not bear to part with it.

But she would think no more about such things. Friday was the magic day. Tonight, Wednesday, and Thursday. She could scarcely contain herself. She wondered whether Andrew was as excited as she was.

She replaced the diary precisely as she had found it, and looked all about the room. She checked the desk once more and again looked at their wedding photo. It was now four o'clock. Should she risk going by Beatrice Brookfield's for tea? The notion excited her. But first she must leave here without attracting attention. She could not go out the front because of Evan, which meant she would have to go to the lower floor and enter the garden. Once there, it would be simple enough to make good a secure departure. Familiarity was her guide and soon she was traversing the last few steps with the happy throbbing of the heart known to the mountain climber. Within a few paces of the rear door, however, there rose a terrible shriek, an angry, startled "Yeeow!" She had stepped on Midnight, invisible on the floor before the door, enjoying the final stages of his afternoon nap. As she leaned down to comfort the cat, the side hall door opened and there was a rush of light. Letitia raised her hand to shield her eyes, but Carolyn's face showed that she had recognized her at once and that she had, like a photographic plate, taken in every detail, which had developed into instant understanding.

"No, no," she whimpered. She broke into sobs as she retreated back into her room, Letitia upon her in a single bound. The expression on Letitia's face was rage, mixed with confusion and fear. Carolyn slipped backward onto her simple cot, her hands clutched tightly over her face to blot out the sight of this deadly apparition. She instinctively knew she would not be allowed to live with her new secret. Cowering, she could not see Letitia's hands surround her throat and be really conscious of the limpness that quickly came as the life-giving air was denied her. Midnight expressed no interest in the affair, contenting himself with licking his insulted tail. Satisfied that the deed was accomplished, Letitia stepped back from the enormity of what she had done. Sweat stood on her forehead, her eyes flashed and her mouth salivated. She leaned against the wall, heavily, and could hear Amanda and Fowler call back and forth in their low melodious voices, which in the softness was love. She struggled to control the lust for the still warm blood of the dead girl and was successful. For she saw in one awful illuminating moment, a flash of conspiracy, how she could still save herself and doom Evan. After all, he had had his opportunity with her. Had they married, obviously things would have been different. He deserved no better fate!

She ripped off Carolyn's simple cotton underclothing, and threw them in the corner. She picked up the frail body and took it to the closet, where with a leather belt she fashioned a noose and hung Carolyn from a hook. Carolyn's tongue seemed swallowed in her open mouth, but the tight belt covered nicely the dull bruises of strangulation. She removed her plain turquoise ring. Next, she tore the blanket off the bed and rumpled the sheets. She took an initialed letter opener, a silver letter opener from the neatly organized desk, but did not disturb the writing pad and pencils. Then she picked up Midnight, extinguished the light, and went back into the hall, where she deposited the cat.

Now outside, she walked across the gravel and then the cement portion of the alleyway to the boundary line between their own and Evan's property. She snapped a few small azalea branches, leaving them hang. She repeated this on two other bushes. She dropped the ring in the grass, on the shortest way to the back door of Evan's house. Then she walked with great care along the azaleas, until she reached the rear garden gate, and then noiselessly she slipped into the park.

She was nervous and excited and tired, and she wanted to cry and she wanted help. She looked about wildly and moved on toward the cemetery. Had she looked more closely, behind the shaking and quaking boxwood hedge, she would have discovered Chauncey Dawson who had spent a damp hour behind the house, settling for a curtailed nap in order to try to validate his theory. He could scarcely credit his eyes when he saw Letitia come directly out of the gate and head toward the cemetery. He started to rise to follow her, but instead he leaned against a maple, waiting for the palpitations of his heart to cease, and for the file system of his clearing brain to sort out this new development. His first step was a false one, catching his right foot in a gopher hole. But finally he righted himself and started off gamely into the growing darkness of the woods.

5

The Finger Points

Beatrice Brookfield had fretted through most of the day. It had rained again—how often could it rain in one city, which was not located geographically in the tropics?—and it was Tuesday, still four days from the ball. Would it always be like this, that she would live from one ball to the next, from one entertainment to the next? She was, after all, eighteen years old and while she could not simply remark them as eighteen years of no excitement, still she could hardly credit them with being more than the delay before growing up, before finding her own way in the world. While it was true that her father's status in society had contributed to a pleasant life, one of leisure, a reasonable education, and above all "expectations," it had none-theless left her in a state of melancholy. She did not know why. But the prospect of coming to America had pleased her immensely, and in some way had promised to end her ennui. She had anticipated the vigor and directness of the American frontier, and instead, had found the men at least pale carbons of London men, with even less initiative, tempered by a certain awe of one of her rank. Where in the world was there really democracy? What did it mean in terms of love and romance?

There had been one positive note, however, and that had been the dinner the previous evening at the Lockhart home. Not only had her host taken an open interest in her, but the doctor, Evan Thomas, who had called before at their home in response to Sir William's stomach maladies, had seemed genuinely envious, proving again the maxim that if it rains, it pours. It was almost 4:30 in the afternoon. Tea time had been a disappointment; neither the fey girl nor Bishop Nestor had shown up. But all was far from lost. Dr. Thomas would be stopping by at five p.m. to minister to Sir William, who even now was in his bed of pain and gastric upset. She worried about her father's health—her fragile mother had passed from the scene in the mists of childhood—and considered herself blessed that her own health was robust and vigorous. And someday she would put that all to good use. There was an appropriateness of timing in all things, the Bible confirmed, and so she would concentrate her thoughts on other things.

The prospects of improving her mind had been greater in America than she had first expected, given the discovery of the slow pace of fascinating events. Still, she had replaced *Le Morte d'Arthur* with Trollope's *Barchester Towers*. Matters of the church had never before seemed to her to be the proper raw material for humor, but she was soon into the intrigue of the plot. Perhaps she would pass it along to Bishop

Nestor. As she remembered, his face was more often droll than smiling, and perhaps the book would cheer him up. On the other hand, perhaps he did not wish to be cheered up. There are people who prefer to go through life in a mode of suffering, perhaps with the notion that so positioned, nothing of a really bad nature will dare approach them.

Her mild philosophic musings were sufficient to divert her eye from the page, and to see out on the Lockhart lawn a young lady playing a form of hopscotch, going from one stone to the next, now dipping like a humming bird into the bushes and then back, and in a burst of grace, disappear altogether to the rear of the garden. This was not so remarkable in itself, perhaps, except that the woman was certainly the one with whom she had an acquaintance, the one who had accompanied her last week on the shopping trip. Her putative tea guest! It was at once astounding and annoying. She had said nothing about where she lived, but surely not next door.

Beatrice rose from her chaise longue and looked over the veranda railing. The rear door of the Lockhart house was closed, and there was no sign of anyone outside. She looked up toward the front where Mr. Lockhart's bedroom was, but there was no sign of light. Was he there, perhaps, by himself, or more salaciously, in the embrace of a demimonde acquaintance? He was an interesting man. It had been bold of her to mention the reception. He had seemed interested, but nonetheless he had said nothing. Some one of the junior officers at the Embassy would probably be assigned to her as a matter of duty. She had had her share of that. Perhaps she would plead illness, and have Evan by in her father's absence to administer to her needs. She stretched again and smiled, realizing all too well what those needs were and how intensely she felt them. Just thinking about those things brought a warmth to her which finally settled between her thighs and left her with a moist feeling. She touched herself ever so lightly, and then walked languidly to her bedroom, where she lay aside her silken wrapper and then went into the bathroom where she slipped into the already warm and scented waters where she would relax and dream until it was time to meet Dr. Thomas when he came to attend to her father.

The rise of Chauncey Dawson from the brush was a miracle no less astounding than the proliferation of fish during the Sermon on the Mount. He somehow recognized, through the intuition of greed, that his $5,000 was fleeing through the grayness of the park. And so, once clear of the gopher hole, like an aging bloodhound, he loped off in pursuit of the trail of the lady in gray. Within a few minutes, he came up against the cast iron barrier posed by the Oak Hill cemetery. Yet it could not block out his view that rounding a sheltered corner of a magnificent and at once dignified crypt was the figure of the gray lady that had just flitted by him. To mount the low stone wall at the juncture of the cemetery and the Brookfield home was, even for Chauncey, the work of an instant, and he traversed the downhill angle with the agility of a mountain goat. And so, peeping from behind a lilac bush, he was the witness to the strangest sober sight of his life, namely this divine creature in her somber, sensuous dress standing by the entrance of a crypt, her eyes high to heaven, her lips moving in some kind of supplication—all this in view at one moment, and at the very next, vanished, a dead leaf from the past.

Had Chauncey been a lesser man, one not steeled

by the Civil War, the detective service with Union Pacific in the West, and outrageous harrassment from the law, he would have stumbled for the gate of the cemetery, opening on R Street, and allowed his quest to end. Yet he did not do any such thing; instead, giving free rein to his curiosity and his greed, he moved toward the crypt and within a minute stood before its gate, exactly where the apparition had stood only seconds before. His heart stuttered again, for he sensed that the lady he had seen in his humble quarters was identical to the furtive lady in gray who had, for her own reasons, skipped quickly from Andrew Lockhart's residence to the somber setting of the resting place of the certified dead.

Chauncey stood back from the iron gate and absorbed the plaque of bronze embedded in the granite. "Ellicott." It was ominous to the viewer, in the same sense as the imprecations of the Pharoahs, warning friend and foe alike to advance no further into the secrets of the dead. It was with difficulty, however, that Chauncey was able to gain this intelligence on his own, and after he pocketed his magnifying glass, he was still left with the impression that neither the crypt itself nor the warning had anything to do with this remarkable lady now in gray. She had sworn his protection; she was like an angel of mercy. Perhaps she was offering prayers on the anniversary of a family death. He leaned against the gate. He shook it gently, but it only rattled in the lock.

Despite waiting on the graveled walk, his shoes talking to each other as he rocked back and forth, there was no sign of the gray lady. He was ordinarily not a superstitious man, but at the same time, he was convinced that he had seen what he had actually seen. He became frightened. He removed his bowler with difficulty, and held it in his hands, like a beggar's bowl. In this pose, head bowed and bowler humbled, he proceeded in a shuffling step toward the exit. And he was calm when he felt the hand on his arm, and an Irish voice announce, "Sir, you are under arrest."

At five o'clock precisely Evan Thomas secured his medical bag, opened the front door of his Federal home, and walked down the five steps to the sidewalk. The street was not as busy as it had been earlier, the merchants having done their duty and the various animals having found their way to security or slaughter closer to the river front. He walked the few paces to the home of the British minister. He was preoccupied in part by the mysteries of the Lockhart house, the familiar face in the window. The remainder of his interest and attention was still on the unsolved murders and he was trying to think it through from fresh perspectives. He had begun the "What if" game and found it endlessly fascinating. Now it had to be interrupted in order to make his professional call on Sir William Brookfield. To his pleasure and surprise, Beatrice answered the door.

"Good evening, Dr. Thomas. The servants are temporarily away and I did not want you to ring in vain."

Beatrice was gorgeous, newly-bathed and full of the fragrance that God had granted mortals. Evan smiled, and a lump rose and disappeared in his throat. After checking Sir William's fever and refilling his paragoric prescription from the stock in his medical bag, Evan found Beatrice waiting in the hallway.

"Do you have time for a little sherry?" she asked, and led him down the hall skirting her bedroom, entering onto the veranda at the east side. She had already poured the Spanish wine into small crystal goblets and resumed her place on the chaise lounge. Evan pulled up a comfortable wrought iron chair. The door to her bedroom was discreetly open. One could see the appurtenances through the friendly window.

"And how is Father?" Beatrice asked, replacing her glass on the low table.

"His stomach is better, but he complains of difficulty in breathing easily. I fear that the climate does not agree with him."

"It is indeed warmer and more muggy than I should have imagined."

"I have not yet suggested to Sir William that he repair to the mountains, say to the Greenbriar in Virginia. A few weeks there would in all probability bring him around."

"That would be fine . . . although I suppose he would want me to go with him."

"You don't find the climate then too enervating?"

"Not really," said Beatrice. Evan seemed to be more at ease than when he first came onto the veranda, the intimacy of the growing dusk and the gray clouds seeming to press them together, however slightly.

"The view is quite lovely from here," said Evan. "You have a superb garden. I fear my own is in disrepair."

"Actually, I rather like the more natural appearance that the lilacs and azaleas present along that side of the Lockhart property. Or is that yours?"

"I'm afraid I am the culprit. And Andrew is about so little that he has never complained. He rather lost interest after—"

At that moment there materialized on the Lockhart lawn, just off the terrace, two dark, thin men, dressed in black suits and wearing bowlers. They were studying the ground carefully, as though someone had lost something small. One uttered a cry and held up something between his fingers, apparently a ring.

"That's odd," said Evan, rising to his feet and going to the railing. "Police, I'd wager."

Beatrice was now by his side, watching the two intruders. "I believe you are right, but what in the world are they doing?"

"I have you as witness that they found something in my yard."

"The fatal bit of evidence."

"Probably a bit of jewelry that will provide the key to my long lost family fortune."

By now the men were near the natural fence created by the bushes and studied that area with a good deal of attention, looking about and up at Evan's house, and finally affixing pieces of string at two places on the bushes. One disappeared and then returned with a lighted lantern against the growing dusk. They then proceeded slowly all along the hedge toward the rear wall. The light showed each of the men alternatively as it swung in front of one, then the other, giving the impression of a giant lightning bug floating over the dark grass.

A gas lamp was lighted in Beatrice's bedroom and tuned down to a low glow. Her personal Negro servant, Rachel, stepped out onto the veranda, closing the bedroom door against the evening insects. Her silver bracelet chimed against a small silver tray filled with thin cucumber sandwiches and salted walnuts. It was a portion of the tea that had been aborted. Rachel left the tray on the table and quietly disappeared through the door at the end of the veranda. Her face had been dull and implacable and she seemed worried. Beatrice had asked her to serve the snacks exactly at six, which would then assure some uninterrupted moments, but the presence of the police and the sense that something was wrong took the slight flush of the sherry and anticipation off the evening. Evan remained standing at the railing, his drink in hand.

"I should not like to intrude," he said at last, "but perhaps it would be best if I went by Andrew's to see if there is anything I can do to help."

"A physician's life is not his own."

"No, I find my private practice, as opposed to my teaching, gets in the way of life's pleasures."

He looked at her curiously, as though he could see inside her mind and read her thoughts. She was not surprised, then, that as he put down the sherry and stepped toward the door, he gathered her quickly into his arms and kissed her, firmly, passionately. Then he walked with her to the door of the veranda and stepped into the hall.

"Thank you so much for such a pleasant interlude. I hope that soon we can try it once more, under more favorable circumstances. . . . Please don't bother. I can find my way to the door."

"No, no. I'll come with you." Beatrice clutched his hand and smiled into his face. "Extending the pleasure even a few more minutes is something I should not readily sacrifice."

Evan was smiling too, placing his finger over his lips as they passed Sir William's room, then on down the narrow stairway toward the high-ceilinged hall. Just inside the door, presenting his card to Rachel, was Captain Eric Logan. The gas lamp high on the wall cast his face in shadow, adding to the usual solemnity of his appearance. Evan preceded Beatrice down the last several steps and shook hands warmly with Logan, although Beatrice felt a certain embarrassment seep through Captain Logan's mein, as though he knew he were interrupting something private and important. Or it might have been his knowledge that the bourbon fumes were noticeable in the hot hallway. He managed a weak smile upon being introduced to her, and she showed Evan and Logan directly to the drawing room. She stood hesitantly, uncertain as to whether to excuse herself in the interests of the men's conversation, but then sat down quietly when Captain Logan, his face a troubled tangle of crevices, motioned her to a seat.

Neither she nor Evan spoke and for a short time it seemed as though Logan would have nothing to say either. At last he began to talk, but not before he was prepared, not before he had checked to his own satisfaction the likely progress of the whole conversation. He was plainly not interested in going into the unknown, if it were necessary. If it had depended upon him, America would not have been discovered.

"Now there has been some difficulty next door at Lockhart's," he said. "Something very tragic."

"I beg your pardon, but I'm intruding, I fear." Bishop Nestor materialized from the adjoining dining room.

"I think not," replied Logan. "As a matter of fact, Bishop, it is fortuitous that you have come along. You may be of service. I want to tell you all what is happening, and seek your advice. This matter is most confidential and I must swear you all to the strictest secrecy."

Along with the gravity in the shaking of heads and the spirit of cooperation exuding from Captain Logan's audience was an electric spark of tension that excited Beatrice. Or was it because she was looking at Evan in a new light? There was something physical and sensual in their exchange of glances and for awhile she found it difficult to keep her mind on the conversation at hand.

Finally Logan said, "There has been a murder committed next-door, a particularly vicious murder."

The Bishop interrupted the filling of his briar to clasp his hemlock crucifix, and moved his lips in a kind of incantation.

"And the pattern?" asked Evan, alert and hopeful.

"Different. Quite different indeed."

"There were no puncture marks?"

"No, it was strangulation. The murderer, however, wanted to leave another impression, apparently. He wanted to provide strong clues that the poor victim, Andrew's maid Carolyn, had been assaulted and then from a sense of shame, had hung herself in her closet."

"But that was not the case?"

"No, I think not." Logan looked about the room at each person, spreading his accusation evenly. The clues leading to Evan, the broken twigs in the hedge and the ring seemed to be a plant. Yet Evan was the only one, to his knowledge, who might have guessed that Carolyn was a police informant.

"And what about other clues?" asked Evan.

"There are a few, which I shall mention later. But what I would like to ask is whether either of you," indicating with his glance Evan and Beatrice, "noticed anyone or anything unusual about the Lockhart home, say, around four-thirty to five."

"Not I," replied Evan. "I was puttering about the house, here and there, out in the garden, a spell on the stoop, and well, nothing really. Restless, I guess. Anyway, at five I came here to call on Sir William to see how he was coming along. I was having a sherry on the veranda with Lady Beatrice about five-thirty when we noticed the two officers in the rear, searching about, and concluded that something was amiss. I was on my way to check into it with Andrew."

"Mr. Lockhart is not at home," said Logan. "The servants claim to have seen nothing."

He frowned at his notebook and jotted a note or two on the pad. He raised his eyes inquisitively, settling on Beatrice.

"Well, I have this to offer," said Beatrice. "At about four-thirty or so, I was sitting on the veranda, reading, when I noticed a young woman over by the bushes separating the Lockhart garden from Evan's. She was young and dark and dressed in gray and seemed to be skipping along, in a kind of hopscotch, and she then disappeared out the back of the garden."

"Did you know her? Did you recognize her?"

"I believe so. Except that under these circumstances, I should not like you to accept this as necessarily true. I mean the distance to the other side of the Lockhart garden is considerable, it was rather dark and gloomy and my observation was casual. Still, I had a certain view and a certain impression during that brief moment."

"Of course," said Captain Logan.

"Last week, on Saturday evening, I decided to go into the shopping and market area of Georgetown—just for something to do. I took the carriage and going down N Street toward Wisconsin I noticed a young woman standing by a street lamp, apparently looking to hail a hansom. I impulsively asked the driver to stop and I invited the woman to ride with me. She accepted gratefully and we spent perhaps two hours together. We got along rather well, in fact, and having few friends here, as of this moment," Beatrice said, her eyes moving toward Evan, "I invited her to tea today. But she didn't come."

"And what was her name?"

"She simply said that her name was Maria, and in the context of the moment, I thought no further about it. Nor did I ask her where she lived, since she did not volunteer that information. I simply assumed she lived somewhere in this vicinity."

"And could you describe her more specifically?"

"Yes. I should say she was about five feet four inches tall, less than six stone—say about one hundred-fifteen pounds—very dark black hair, black, almost luminous eyes, a pinkish complexion, a good figure, dainty feet."

"And what was she wearing?"

"Then she was wearing a white taffeta dress, over a crinoline or two, purple ribbons about the neck and sleeves. Today she was wearing something gray and flowing, rather formless."

"And she told you nothing about herself, things she had done, places she had been, things she planned to do?"

"She seemed interested in buying a piece of jewelry for a man. I don't know for what occasion. We visited several shops, but bought nothing."

Evan had sat mesmerized as he heard Beatrice's account of her woman friend. He sat stiffly in his chair as though made of stone. Then he became slightly red, as though he were having trouble breathing or something had caught in his throat. Logan had now finished taking down the notes of Beatrice's narrative. He had become introspective, leaning back in his chair. Rachel arrived carrying a silver tea service and passed around cups and saucers filled with savory Indian tea. While the good Logan pondered, the rest of the assembly, including Evan, added the sugar and lemon, and sipped and thought their own thoughts. Logan was clearly trying to piece together some odds and ends.

Before her murder, Carolyn had been seated at the tiny desk, starting a report of her findings to be handed over to the police. It had been sketchy and then had been broken off in mid-sentence.

On the surface, the household goes on at a normal pace. Mr. Lockhart works late and rises early. When he is not at his office in town, he spends a good deal of time in his bedroom, writing and studying the stars with his telescope, which is in a glass-enclosed room leading from the study. The only thing that has aroused my suspicions is that the closet across the way is about half full of a woman's clothes—I assume that they are of the late Mrs. Lockhart—and from time to time the order appears changed, not, certainly, by me. At night I sometimes hear a shuffling sound in the hall, near the closet. Sometimes that is accompanied by exceptionally loud purring of the cat, which stays in this part of the house as well as in the carriage house. Perhaps more—

All that was fine so far, supporting the idea of unidentified activity of some sort. There was something odd about the house which Logan had noticed for years as he had become familiar with the neighborhood. That is why he had not hesitated to send Carolyn there under the guise of a maid when an anonymous letter, pasted together from newspaper headline letters, had urged him to do so. The trouble was that there was nothing specific enough yet for Logan to get his hands on.

In the meantime, despite the tea, Evan was in a high state of agitation and now Logan finally noticed it. Surely he was not guilty of this terrible murder.

The clues were so clumsy. But Logan would let him suffer for a bit. True, the maid/informant's murder was of a different pattern, suggesting that there were two murderers instead of one, and that was untidy. He was not completely satisfied that the first two were solved, but he would give up on his theory of the suction device only under the greatest duress. After all, the suspect was now in the jail and the device itself was hard evidence.

"What do you think of Lady Beatrice's observation, Evan?"

He struggled for control, as though he wanted to say a good deal, but finally thought better of it. "I don't really know what to say."

"You didn't see the person?"

"No."

"You were quite by yourself?"

"Yes."

"This new murder comes as a special shock," said Captain Logan. "I thought we were in the process of wrapping up the entire package."

"You have progressed that far?" asked the Bishop.

"There is a certain unsavory tramp whose trail leads all over these cases. He works in a barbershop as a janitor but spends most of his time—whatever time is left over from his bouts with the demon rum—trying to cadge work as a detective. The jobs he gets in that line are not for discussion here, and in any event make no difference. He approached Mrs. Woodward to help solve her daughter's murder, which made us suspicious in the first instance. Next, in searching his quarters, we came upon a rubber hose with a needle valve."

Evan nodded sagely. The significance of that piece of equipment, the missing implement, was such as to require no comment from the cognoscenti. "And then, just a while ago, we found him in the Oak Hill cemetery, incoherent."

"That would seem to do it, then," said Evan.

"I had thought so, until the latest development," replied Logan. "I should be pleased if he confesses. So far, he won't confess anything. He just talks of a dark and luminous lady, such as you describe, Lady Beatrice, coming out the rear garden gate, and that he was in the process of following her when she disappeared among the markers and the crypts of Oak Hill cemetery."

"Still, he was nearby," said Evan. "That is, he might have had the opportunity to have also murdered the maid."

"True, but for the moment I'm putting that idea to one side. It doesn't fit into the pattern. But what about this woman, this luminous woman? We'll have to start tracking her down. It should not be too difficult."

"I cannot agree with that," said Evan, perspiring freely on the forehead. "There is great difficulty in my own mind in accepting the description of the woman." His mouth worked about and his voice had an unnatural huskiness.

"Why is that?" asked Beatrice in all innocence.

"Because the person you describe would seem to be Letitia, Andrew's wife, who died last December."

This extraordinary statement had the force of a physical blow. Captain Logan was the first to recover. "I would assume, Evan, that what we are dealing with is not a superstitious notion, but a case of mistaken identity, with which I am familiar. Yet I can see that you are serious and I respect you as a professional."

Bishop Nestor puffed quietly on his pipe, and in the

midst of this shock and confusion, all eyes turned toward him.

"Tell me, Bishop," said Evan in a voice full of pleading, "can the dead return? Is there some process that makes such an otherwise preposterous thing possible?"

"The notion is ancient and complex and is the subject of much learned study as well as controversy. Actually I would much prefer not to get involved in it, but since you have asked me and are obviously perplexed, I shall. In my opinion, the short answer is yes. This assumes, mind you, that the person really did not die, but was really an Un-Dead, which is quite a different thing. I see now your concern over the puncture marks. Yes, I do accept the argument that there are vampires. This does not square with the dogma of most churches, so one ordinarily keeps one's views to oneself. It is after all a universal superstition which must, at some point, be based in fact."

"Let's follow your point for a moment," said Logan. "I happen to believe to the contrary." There was a general nodding of heads in support of his position. "How, for instance, would one become a vampire?"

"First causes? Ah, one must always start with a miracle of sorts. Man has stubbornly resisted the natural progression, from the womb to the tomb, and the search for elixirs and fountains of youth is large in our recorded history. The peculiar circumstance of a kind of disease, a fever, human blood, and unsanctified earth apparently works on occasion. The body is thus kept alive and retains the custody of the soul and is the main reason why theologians generally find vampirism so unattractive."

"Just as do people generally."

"There is of course great fear because of the vampire's blood lust, which often increases in the course of this kind of life. Vampires are not all the same; they have different characteristics, just like people. If they all looked alike, it would be a simple matter to exterminate them. Once a vampire is recognized as such, it is a matter of tracking it to its resting place where it meets its common fate: a stake through the heart and the severing of the head, stuffing the mouth with garlic. The soul is thereby released."

"I see," said Logan. "But what of their movements? This person was sighted during the day, and I had understood, insofar as I have read or heard anything about this kind of thing at all, that the vampire is inert, helpless in its box by day and is only at large at night."

"Again relying on ancient texts, not necessarily. A vampire can appear during the day, especially cloudy and dark days, but without the ability of transmogrification, that is, without the power to turn themselves into a bat or even a wolf. Still, they may be able to undergo some kinds of physical change. Generally, in the day, they are less awesome but are still very powerful."

"Powerful enough to strangle someone and hang them up like a garment in a closet?"

"Yes, indeed. I should say so."

"How is it that you have learned so much about vampires?" asked Beatrice.

"It is my trade or profession to deal with things spiritual, with the soul, and so to the extent that vampires are partly of the spirit, they have come into my purview."

"And you have no doubts about the existence of the soul?" asked Evan.

"Indeed no," smiled the Bishop. He sipped some tea

before once again picking up his evil-smelling briar. "In all beliefs, since primitive days, the soul is independent of the body. Most simply put, the primitive mind—and the modern mind as well, I might add—could not understand the animation process, that is, why man or animal moved. The most satisfactory explanation seemed to be that a smaller specimen identical to the larger one, if we study Egyptian archeological artifacts, for example, moves the larger. When a fox runs, he is propelled by an identical, tiny fox. For the ancients, when a man sleeps, it was not unreasonable for them to think that the soul might be out traveling elsewhere, as a bee or a butterfly. This accounts for the taboo against suddenly awakening a sleeping person for fear his soul would not be back."

Captain Logan nodded. All these preachers were quite alike, whatever their rank, he thought. Give them an inch. . . . "I can accept your faith in the existence of a separate soul. I think I believe that myself. But the matter of the vampire, about which you seem to speak with equal conviction, I find impossible to accept. We will find a simpler solution, I'm sure, closer to home."

"I would prefer your logic, Logan . . . but I am almost persuaded that I too have seen Letitia, recently, in the evening in Andrew's garden," said Evan.

Logan's face reddened. "I feel I have fallen into a spell of sorts. How easily we talk about vampires as though they exist. Now, I am open-minded. I do not mind discussing information that defies reason. But it is nothing but that. I more readily accept the notion of mistaken identity. With this description, we shall soon find this person. The investigation will continue in a more profitable, and I may add, sensible direction."

"Where does this leave matters then?" asked Evan.

"The tramp in jail has been charged with the two murders in the park. The evidence of the hose, plus his approach to the Woodwards and his proximity to the events should be sufficient to persuade a jury."

"You prefer a bird in the hand to a vampire?" asked Evan.

"Yes," replied Logan, "a bird to a bat."

"But what about the murder of Andrew's maid?"

"Following the same logic, I must come down on the side of the physical and not the spiritual, with no offense intended, Bishop," said Logan.

"Each man to his own calling," said the Bishop. "The law provides scant weight to the case for the supernatural, the occult as they might call it, even though the practitioners of the law would, probably to a man, say that their faith in the existence of the human soul was very much intact. The Vampire, to my mind, is really the best evidence of the existence of the human spirit."

"In other words, Captain, you are at a loss on this murder. Perhaps I should examine the body in more detail, if it has not already been done."

"The body is in the morgue for an autopsy, and I regret that you shall not be of assistance."

"I am willing, as always, to do it at no charge to the District."

"It is not that, Doctor," said Captain Logan rising. "The only clues that we have make you the principal suspect. You or the vampire. Which would you choose? There are broken twigs on bushes between the two property lines, indicating that someone passed through. And a ring, a simple turquoise ring, which belonged to the maid, was found in the grass—on your lawn."

"I am absolutely innocent," said Evan.

"The notion that Evan had anything to do with

murder is absurd, Captain," said Beatrice in a tone of alarm and disbelief.

"I am not pressing charges, because I do not believe Evan is guilty either. Yet sooner or later the case will be decided on evidence, and it shall be the evidence which shall decide the question of guilt."

"The real evidence is all about you," cried Evan, "but you refuse to see it."

Evan buried his head in his hands in an attitude of guilt. No, of despair. No one would believe him, despite the eloquence of the Bishop and the description provided by Beatrice. What would have to happen before Logan would act?

6

The Love Fest

The short, late afternoon rest restored Letitia's spirits momentarily but not her strength. Outside the crypt she felt dejected. For a long time in her nocturnal forays, which were hardly innocent pleasures, she had felt nothing stronger or more disturbing than remorse. Now the notion of guilt bore down on her and it was with difficulty that she struggled against it. She feared facing Andrew, for she knew he would be furious with her. "How am I to take you away from here safely if you won't behave, if you embroil us in this terrible scandal just when I have almost completed all the arrangements, right down to the hour and day? How could you do it?" Did he have any relationship with the dead Carolyn, had there been something there that she had not noticed? In that case he might be ashamed and blame the whole affair on himself. It was common currency that most men prefer only one type of woman, that if there is a second wife, she will have a marked resemblance to the first. The prudent thing to do, she thought, was to go by the house as a mist, to see what the police were doing, whether Andrew was at home. He might be understanding, after all. But what could she have done? If she had not killed Carolyn, all their future plans would have been so much rubble.

She moved slowly through the cemetery, like a shadow among the tombstones and trees. The moon's glow was dimmed behind the slow moving, ponderous clouds. She still felt tired physically, and she knew the only answer to that condition. Soon the blood lust would be upon her and she could do nothing at all until she had satisfied it. The houses along Q Street were shuttered, as though the inhabitants did not want to look out on the night. Until the solution to the park murders was announced, and now that of the maid, who could blame them? Yet it made her task all the more difficult. There was not a child on the street, and in the distance, the only people she could see were in small groups. Preoccupied with these thoughts, she was within several doors of Andrew's house when she realized her double peril. First, there were definitely police stakeouts in front of the house, discreet shadows along the big maples. Second, she felt so weak that she feared that she could not carry out the transmogrification successfully, that the physical and psychic strength required was not within her. Above all she felt lonely, an outcast from her former bright world, a kind of criminal, through no fault of her own, an object of disgust which every booted foot would grind into the dirt without a single word of pity. But for a friend. That single note raised her spirit. Perhaps Beatrice Brookfield was at home. It had been kind of

Beatrice to invite her to tea after such a brief acquaintance. It was true that they had mutually enjoyed the shopping trip, were comfortable with each other. Had it not been for the unfortunate Carolyn incident, she might have gone. Still, from Beatrice's point of view, her failure to show up or to send regrets was simply rude. She did not want Beatrice to think poorly of her. She could come by even now ostensibly to apologize. That was a good enough reason. It was scarcely ten, too early, surely, for her yet to have retired.

Like the other handsome Federal houses in this block, the home occupied by Sir William was almost flush on the street, only five brick steps leading to the sidewalk. The street was paved with bricks and was a preferred passage for the carriages and commercial drays, but there was no one in sight save the shadows along the streets. Letitia pondered whether she might work her way around to the back and enter from the garden, but she was convinced that police might well be stationed there too. She had realized that Chauncey Dawson must have positioned himself in that area, for she had noticed him just as she had entered the crypt. If he could conceal himself, then it was simple indeed. There was no way out of it, then, except to become one with the air and float along the feeble moonbeams, along the second floor of the brick house, tightly shuttered along the east side where Sir William's quarters were located. The Bishop Nestor occupied the third floor bedroom. The arrangement of the interior of the house, in fact, was not dissimilar to Andrew's. How sad it was that when she recalled her own home, she could no longer attach her own identity to it.

The veranda was empty. Letitia reappeared and sat

down wearily on the chaise longue. She left weak and lay back on the seat as Beatrice had done earlier in the day. The chair where Evan had sat had been preserved in its place by Beatrice in a sentimental gesture, designed, she hoped, to insure another visit soon from the man who was now the center of her heart's interest. Letitia had no way of knowing she was interfering with Beatrice's totem when she moved from the chaise longue to the chair, changing its orientation so that she could observe Beatrice's actions through the window, discreetly and safely.

Beatrice was lying on the bed, clad in a rose-colored nightgown of a gossamer-like material. The sheet was pulled down to the foot of the bed, where it could be recalled toward dawn if the cool of the night fell on the sweltering city. She seemed restless and fitful, from time to time sighing, as the moonlight coming in from the east window. There was the possibility that it would be clear tomorrow, thought Letitia, which meant that she must remain in the crypt, for the bright sunlight left her weak and she had barely regained the earth box safely on one occasion when she had rashly tested it. What should she do now? Should she call out to Beatrice, inviting her to join her on the veranda? Suddenly there was a cooling breeze from the north and west and a rustle among the magnolias that stood at the west wing of the veranda. Yes, it was going to be fair tomorrow. But what if her presence frightened Beatrice and she cried out? Letitia crept closer to the half-open door where she could see better. Beatrice had pulled the sheet up onto her body. Her head stirred on the pillow as she made herself comfortable in the enclosing arms of Morpheus. Letitia felt a shudder pass through her own body, and the hypnotic pink haze began to exude from her as she began to glide toward the bed. Letitia quivered in an almost uncontrollable agitation. The whole appearance of the room—the cut flowers, the canopy over the bed, the sitting arrangement of low, overstuffed chairs and a well-polished walnut table by the single, large window to enjoy the morning view—all this gave the room a kind of bridal atmosphere, which Letitia remembered well. Could she have enjoyed the honeymoon more if she had known her fate? Probably. They could have continued on from New York to some forgotten place in Europe and never set eye on the Vampire. Yet Letitia refused to yield to fantasy. There was a strange attraction about this scene growing within her that was demanding expression. Beatrice stirred under the sheets of the expansive bed. Her form was outlined in the dim light. Her shoulders were bare against the edge of the pillow.

Letitia advanced slowly, quietly, in a faint haze that covered the immediate vicinity of the bed, where she stopped. Beatrice's eyes were closed in sleep, but fluttered momentarily as Letitia bent over her. Slowly and skillfully, Letitia began pulling the sheet down from Beatrice's still figure, revealing the flat pink stomach where the nightgown had already risen in her brief restlessness, then the mount of Venus, which already was lending its special perfume to the heavy, moist air. Finally, Beatrice lay open before her dark visitor, her legs bent in an invitation to love, her hips moving in sleepy sensuous rhythm. As Letitia bent over the bed, the dark clouds regained their mastery of the moon. The smells and aroma began to drive her into a frenzy. She recognized that she was contributing to the perfume of lust that hung over the scene. There was delight and imagery in her mind as she thought of the splendor of the bedroom she had so recently shared with Andrew. After a few moments, Beatrice quivered in a long, sensuous shudder. Her breathing quickened, and her sighs increased. Then there was a stronger almost overpowering aroma of her sex.

Letitia, now giddy and weak, removed her own taffeta and the crinolines, placed them neatly over the back of the chair, and removed her shoes and underclothes, leaving them in a tidy pile under the chair. Beatrice's legs made a kind of cradle. Letitia began rubbing her calves with the tips of her fingers, in a softly rolling motion. She could feel the complete relaxation of the muscles as she proceeded to the inner thighs. The musk-like smell of Beatrice's sex was now joined by Letitia's. Despite herself, she was aroused to a feverish warmth by this phase of her enterprise.

The breeze quickened from the open casement, riffling the gossamer of Beatrice's rumpled gown like a tiny wave on a pond. Letitia softly kissed the inside of Beatrice's thighs, now moist with her own effluence. Beatrice responded with more sighs and a moan of pleasure and Letitia opened her sex like a flower, and then like a bee going from petal to petal, at last settled on the pistil; with low sucking sounds and a light tongue she aroused in Beatrice the greatest of erotic pleasure and soon felt her trembling. Feeling her own moisture growing, Letitia began to knead Beatrice's breasts and at the same moment, sink her incisors into the labia and feel the sweet trickle of blood move down her tongue into her throat. She placed her hands under Beatrice's buttocks and slowly moved her hips. Beatrice obliged by raising her thighs, comforting Letitia's face and sighing ecstatically as the process of love went on.

All through the night the whippoorwills sang, and from far off, there were the occasional calls of the owl.

Then the nervous twitter of the cardinal, growing restless before the dawn. Like Beatrice, Letitia was in a languid state and it was with difficulty that she finally raised her satiated red lips from Beatrice's. Letitia felt a great new tranquility and a state of well-being. She had never taken so much blood from Andrew, out of concern for his eventual future. But she had no such worry about Beatrice. She would recover. She would be safe enough once Letitia left. She smiled to herself somewhat greedily. It was nice to think that she had her all to herself and a shame that she would be leaving so soon, now that they had gotten to know each other better, albeit under the cover of night. Perhaps Letitia could visit her once again, as a kind of farewell.

The sheet below the scene of the love feast was heavily spotted with blood. She went into the commode and wiped the smear of blood from her lips and cheeks and dropped the towel to the cool tile floor. She dressed quickly and quietly. The moon had gone, and the false light of dawn was on the eastern horizon. It was still dark enough, however, for her to rejoin the last layer of night to escape unnoticed toward the crypt.

An instant after she made this transformation, a giant bat came flying to the open window, its red eyes glowing with hate, and blood dripping from its envenomed teeth. It attached its foul feet to the curtain and glowered at Beatrice. It paused for a moment and then seemed to grow larger and with a gigantic wing blocked Beatrice from view. The Master! Letitia streamed through the narrow curtain separating the night from the dawn and with wracking sobs, sought solace in her coffin.

Andrew paced the bedroom floor, hands clasped behind his back, his eyes half-closed in thought. Whatever confusion existed over the unfortunate Carolyn, the case was absolutely clear to him. For one thing, he could smell the odor of gardenias and for the other, the thread inside his private desk drawer, designed to warn him of surreptitious entry, had been broken. While he was no detective, the events of the afternoon were no mystery to him. But were they to Captain Logan?

As both a matter of circumstance and preference, Andrew had not had many dealings with the police. They were a necessary element of society to assure that the rights of the owners of property were protected and respected, but this was to be in the general order of things, a smooth functioning gear in the mechanism of life. While Captain Logan had treated him with the respect due his social and official rank, the whole interview had somehow ended on a dissonant note, as though the middle C in the piano, for example, was not quite in tune.

"And how long has the deceased been in your employ?"

"Two months, no longer than two months."

"And how did you go about securing her services?"

"What do you mean, 'how did I go about—?' "

"I mean, did you place a notice in the newspapers?"

"No, no, she just came 'round and I decided to employ her."

"I see. You had all along needed another servant."

"Yes."

Captain Logan had frowned at his notebook, and Andrew felt a sense of unease coming across his temples. Anything one said to this fellow somehow sounded sinister. Could he divine, by some new device, an inner, sensitive ear, the subtle edge on his replies that showed they were not quite correct? He had hired her as a decoy, but that fact and that act had actually produced, or threatened to produce, the very result he had attempted to avoid.

"During this time, did she ever mention any prowlers, or . . . a feeling of danger of any kind?"

"No, I don't believe so. You might ask Amanda and Fowler, the Negro servants, who were more in her confidence, I believe, than I."

"What of her effects? Were any of them missing?"

"I should have no idea, Captain. I am quite unaware of what she may have brought into the house."

"What of the closet across from her room? Are those clothes hers or . . . ?"

Andrew felt a flush come over his face, as though he had bent over an iron cooking range, glowing red-hot, and he felt the relief as he stepped back. "Clothes . . . what clothes?"

"There seems to be a closet in which there are women's clothes—nice, expensive-looking clothes, in fact—incongruous, perhaps, for one of Carolyn's status. Do you think they could have played any role in the tragedy? Could she have been involved in something to have earned those clothes, or come about them in some other way?"

"I should think not. I think the clothing to which you refer may have belonged to my late wife."

"Your late wife?" asked Captain Logan. "As I understand it she passed away last year. But isn't it customary to give the effects—"

"Indeed, Captain, her personal clothing was given, for the most part, to charity. Something must have been overlooked. I'll have them out of the house tomorrow."

"I'm sorry to have disturbed you, Mr. Lockhart. How you handle the deceased's effects is completely up to you. You see, I'm searching for the possible motivation for this foul play. Carolyn might have bought those items from a fence, for example, and fallen behind in her payments."

"I see," said Andrew.

He had been tardy in disposing of Letitia's things, and when she returned, her first demand was for her finer clothes. Andrew had at that time protested that if she were not careful, someone would notice her comings and goings, and using her wardrobe in her nocturnal adventures as well as possibly alerting the servants would be dangerous. Hence the compromise of the downstairs closet. He had delayed putting his mind to it for too long. Compromise was not really his way.

"And you say you returned home about six?"

"Yes, it was just about that time."

"You did not discover the body?"

"No, Fowler had that unhappy role. You have talked to him about it?"

"Yes, I have."

"I don't think, then, that there is anything more I can offer."

Captain Logan remained thoughtful. They were standing in the drawing room, neither content to sit down for a more leisurely confrontation.

"There is one thing. I should like to be shown through the house."

"Without a search warrant?"

"The murder is all the warrant I need, Mr. Lockhart. Yet if you prefer—"

"Not really. Come this way."

It was only in the master bedroom, however, where Logan seemed to have any particular interest, as though he had had a kind of mental divining rod.

Andrew feared that he would demand to see the contents of the desk, but instead, Captain Logan contented himself with looking closely at the books and photos, especially their wedding photo. The great cedar chest below the double window caught his attention but not his curiosity. No, he bore in on the desk, as though both he and Andrew could envision Letitia sitting there, reciting Byron's poems, inspecting Andrew's diary. Andrew had kept his diary quite faithfully. Perhaps now was the time to consider not only discontinuing the practice, but also destroying what he had. There was no longer any point in meticulously putting into the record what one thought or did. It would be better to have nothing of the kind about.

"This is a pleasant room, Mr. Lockhart," said Logan. "Cool in the evening." Actually it was. The sun was blocked from the south and east by the shade trees and to the west by Evan's house. "And very private," Logan concluded.

At the door to the street, Logan waved a kind of salute and was off into the night. The knowledge that the principal suspect was Evan, thought the Captain, would give Lockhart something to ponder, perhaps set him off in some direction. He was certain that Andrew was concealing something. In the meantime, he had all the men he could spare looking for a slight, dark woman. Beatrice's testimony was being put to good use, and Logan felt they would locate her soon. And if not . . . he shook his head as he headed for the precinct station. Perhaps there would be more facts on hand, some new lead for the case. As for the park murders, he had at least secured Chauncey Dawson in the D.C. jail over by Anacostia. He had been embarrassed to list Evan as a suspect, yet he was as weary of these unexplained crimes as were his superiors. The motive for the crime in the Lockhart house was difficult to conjure. Lockhart himself was confused and reticent, as though he were reluctant to say anything. This kind of uncertainty, a lack of confidence, bemused Logan. People of Lockhart's social status seemed to defy the laws of human nature, which Logan counted on always to resolve life's little mysteries.

Andrew felt distraught. He wished Letitia would come by now, while he was still so provoked and disturbed, angry enough to demand that she remain in the crypt until he advised her what she must do. It was very serious business now. Logan had stated that the suspected murderer of the two in the park had been jailed, yet how had he put it when Andrew had asked for more details? Andrew recalled Logan's exact words: "Because the evidence pointed to him in a variety of ways—he had no witness to account for his whereabouts at the time of the crimes—and besides, no one else stepped forward."

There was a touch of mockery in his voice, Andrew thought, yet he might only be hearing nuances and innuendoes which were not there, but supplied by his own knowledge and suspicion. He felt the guilt himself, really, for not being able to tell Logan what he suspected. Yet it was no more than that at this moment. He did not know for a fact that Letitia had murdered Carolyn. There had been no puncture marks on the throat, according to Fowler under discreet questioning, yet the old retainer may have simply overlooked them in the excitement. He was weary of weighing the right and wrong of everything, whether it were matters of public as opposed to private action, from the question of responsibility, for the suffering Cubans or the tortured Letitia. If he could successfully protect her until Friday, he thought it might all work out. He had reserved a cabin on a steamer from Alexandria to New York. When Letitia again appeared, he would have to speak harshly, or she would spoil the whole plan.

The prospect that the murder might simply go unresolved had for a moment appeared good when Captain Logan expressed his bafflement. When he had told Andrew, however, that his principal suspect was Evan, Andrew had felt ill. He had no doubt that Evan was in no way guilty, but feared that the outrage of the charge would stimulate his survival instinct. There had been times when Andrew thought Evan knew the secret of the house, when he would in a comradely way clap Andrew on the shoulder as though to cheer him up and relieve his melancholy of the winter. There had been more than one night, when the spring evenings crept higher in the hours of the clock, that Andrew had seen Letitia in the street, walking along by herself, mingling with the folk for her own reasons. Evan might well have run into her on occasion. True, her safety was in the fact that no one expected to see her, and Evan above all, for he had pronounced her dead.

It would be nice to leave with the murders solved, so that the name of Lockhart would not be bathed in the light of scandal and suspicion. Just as Andrew was now ready to go, he would be ready to come back, at the proper time. His letter of resignation had been accepted by Mr. Day "with sincere appreciation and regret" and so that avenue was still open, if he wanted to stroll down it again. But he had to take care of Letitia. He loved her, most of all, and knew that she could no longer help herself. What new outrage she might provoke he had no idea, no idea at all. Both Captain Logan and Evan were most assuredly on the alert. It was a very dark night. Andrew would go to the observatory and wait patiently until there was another break in the heavens so that the wonders of the night would once again be visible to him.

The humiliation of it all. Evan fumed at the humiliation of being suspected as a common criminal, a murderer, a would-be rapist. He sat in his study, drinking his brandy neat. His sense of the injustice of the tools of justice, specifically Captain Logan, was so strong that he did not think much of what would happen to his medical career, or to his relationship with Beatrice. He was pleased that she had stoutly defended his innocence. Yes, he would have to pursue her without delay, and without the hesitations that so far had blighted his affairs of the heart. These concerns necessarily would wait until justice was done, and then they would no longer be problems. To be accused falsely of murder was not much different from being buried alive. Even then, if the casket were properly equipped, one could ring the bell above ground by a cord, and have the burial party and the mourners cheerfully reverse the process.

There was but one thought in Evan's mind: Beatrice's innocent description of the lady in gray skipping across the lawn. If one could make that mental leap from the dead to the quick, then the whole scene fell into place. How would one go about proving such a case? The first step, he supposed, would be to convince Captain Logan that the circumstances warranted a court order to inspect the Ellicott crypt. Logan had been willing to listen to Bishop Nestor's rather theoretical and metaphysical explanation of the possibility of people, through a set of circumstances, arriving at an Un-Dead condition, the world of the vampire. Yet it was equally clear that Logan would prefer not to believe it, and officially, he was not willing to recognize such a prospect. And with good reason. After all, these were not the Dark Ages. If Evan could come by evidence, any evidence, on his own, perhaps Logan would obtain an order to open the crypt under some pretext to satisfy his own curiosity, without in the process admitting for an instant that he was such a dunce as to believe in the walking dead. Evan could, for example, go out into the cemetery toward dawn and observe. He shuddered at the thought. Yet doing nothing was an equally great risk for him, suspected as he was of a crime he had not committed. Looked at in that way, the observation in the cemetery was not really foolish or dangerous, assuming that the object of one's search was actually located.

Another brandy strengthened his resolve. He decided to nap right in the study, in his clothes, waking each hour as the hall clock struck. At five he would put his plan into action.

"What's going on down there?" asked Sir William.

"Whatever it was," said the Bishop, "it has now disbanded."

"Now you have my full curiosity," said Sir William. "What was that low mumble all about?"

"The local police inspector, a Captain Logan, came by to report on some trouble next door."

"At that Lockhart fellow's?"

"Yes, one of the servants was murdered."

"Blessed God! We are situated in a treacherous spot. Have they tracked the fellow down?"

The Bishop paused. To tell Sir William that the main suspect was his own doctor simply would not do. "I believe the police officer has a suspect in mind, but there seemed to be precious few clues."

"What about diplomatic immunity?"

"I don't think I understand, Sir William."

"This very house is an extention of England. No one is allowed to enter this place without my permission. If a criminal comes in here, he is violating an international treaty and will suffer the consequences."

"Perhaps that is why these crimes are not spilling over into these premises. But Lady Beatrice provided the officer with some useful information, I do believe, about a mysterious lady who left the Lockhart house shortly after the crime must have been committed."

"She is too young to get involved in this kind of thing, my friend."

"There is no way of course to know whether her observations have any bearing on the murder, although I must say that the doctor, Dr. Thomas, and the police officer paid close attention to what she said and took the whole matter with utmost seriousness."

"And why should they not? Beatrice is an intelligent and forthright girl. And she is my daughter."

"I have put that rather badly," said the Bishop, momentarily embarrassed. "But you are not well. Perhaps we should talk of other things."

"No, confound it! I want to know about what is going on right under my own nose. That's what many people forget. If you don't pay attention to what is going on around you, it is not long until confusion spreads and you don't know anything at all."

"Aside from your health, I'm afraid it would run against the grain of your cynical nature."

"That's what you think, is it? Just because I rarely attend Church?"

"As the shadows lengthen, you'll come back."

"In the end we're all cowards, I suppose."

"At any rate more willing to believe, to believe in the spiritual side of man's nature."

"But what has this to do with the murder, the woman suspect, and so on?"

"Well, considerable, for ultimately it is a matter of belief. It also may mean whether an innocent man is charged for the crime instead of having to put the blame on the guilty party."

"You bishops talk in riddles, I know, to protect yourself from the faithful. Otherwise, they might tear you to pieces."

The Bishop smiled and sucked on his dead pipe. "Your morale has not been diminished by your illness. All right, then, let me put it directly to you: the description by Beatrice of the unknown lady was a description of Lockhart's dead wife."

"That's nonsense."

"I should ordinarily agree, except that the reaction of the two men was quite serious. More of puzzlement than simple incredulity."

"If I understand you correctly, the principal suspect is a spirit, a ghost. How can one deal with that?" Sir William was suddenly overwhelmed with a wracking cough and perspiration stood out on his forehead. Still, he kept the sheet high about his neck, as though he were simultaneously shivering.

"My assumption, Sir William, is that the suspect is most likely to be a vampire."

"Vampire? Such rubbish. Who was that fellow who wrote a book about a vampire? Saw it on the stage. *Dracula.* Stoker, the writer, I do believe. But that was fiction, the work of the imagination, not a real story, you know, nothing like Sir Aurel Stein's stuff."

"The treatment in that book of course was fictional,

119

yet it does not follow that there are no such things as vampires."

"Blood suckers! Certainly there are blood suckers. You chaps should know best of all." Sir William chuckled. "I'm glad you're a bishop and not a police officer."

"No one is more concerned with the human spirit in all its many forms than I am," said the Bishop. "But I fear all this talk is taxing. Here, let me pour you some water."

He helped Sir William raise his head from the pillow, and he drank greedily. The sweat was heavy on his brow and face, and the Bishop wiped him gently with a damp cloth. He also patted up the pillow and generally made him more comfortable. It was in this fashion, as he again laid the tiring knight back on the pillow, that he noticed the two purplish puncture marks on the left side of the throat.

7

The Spit of Pleasure

The stroke of five found Evan quite awake. Wednesday morning. He rose slowly from his leather overstuffed chair, with some stiffness, and prepared to leave. He went to the pantry where he found the lantern. He decided, however, not to take it. He paused over a small piece of apple pie that his cook Sarah had left under a mesh covering. He had earlier decided against carrying his revolver. He did pick up a walking stick, but all in all, he felt foolish going out the back door into the yard and garden, then outside into the damp and quiet park, then east to the low stone cemetery wall that abutted Sir William's residence. At first he felt more foolish than frightened. Yet he was no more over the wall than his heart began beating faster and the calls of the morning birds and even the movement of the ascending clouds startled him. As he tried to focus his eyes to find the pattern of the testimonies to the memory of the fallen, he tripped on a marker and fell heavily. He lost his walking stick.

All over the dark gray of the cemetery there seemed to be movement, the soft noises of the night retreating to their secret hidden places to rest and later reappear. Was this so with the spirit? Bishop Nestor had made a rather compelling case for the existence of the soul, as a separate entity, but once freed from the body, why would the soul have have any more use for it? Except in the case of the vampire. What an extraordinary concept. Evan had on occasion encountered a "green body," that is a corpse which when exhumed was still remarkedly preserved. One of the most famous cases of this kind was the body of Revolutionary War General "Mad Anthony" Wayne who died fighting Indians, and was buried in the hills of Pennsylvania in 1796. When his dutiful son Col. Issac Wayne came thirteen years later to remove his father's bones to the ancestral grave site, at Radnor, Pa., it had been necessary for him to boil the corpse in a huge iron pot so as to remove the flesh from the almost perfectly preserved body. Nonetheless, such tales produced the idea of the dead walking by night, the burying of murderers at crossroads so the spirit would become lost, or even cutting off the head of a suicide to insure that the spirit would behave itself.

It was with his mind filled with such thoughts that he approached the Ellicott family crypt, in fear and fright. His imagination exaggerated every sound and motion, and the pounding of his heart and the quickening alertness of his senses all persuaded him that he was not alone in this graveyard. His reluctant eyes confirmed it; up ahead, there was a movement among the monuments, something coming carefully toward the entrance of the crypt.

Evan froze behind a head-high tombstone. His instinct was to bolt and run, yet his personal interest in a solution to the murder of the maid was great enough to overcome his natural proclivity. He was in a poor position, however, to observe the approaching figure, blending in and out of the gray, now blocked from view altogether by a massive granite marker, now partially in sight. He could make out very little. And if it continued on its present course and entered the crypt, Evan's view would be completely obscured and he would be no wiser than before! He determined then to cut around the back of the crypt and station himself past the entrance on the north side, so he could see the entrance clearly. He accomplished this maneuver successfully within ten minutes, and he began his vigil. The sky to the east was showing signs of light, but the clouds, borne by a westerly wind, seemed to be stacked up like a cinder block wall, delaying the appearance of the mighty chariot of the sun.

Everything he had done to improve his observation of the scene had been perfect, except that the quarry had vanished. He strained his eyes into the gloom and there was not a single movement. Had the person already entered the crypt? That was a possibility that he would examine only after the sun was up and the dark and shadows, which still frightened him, would be dispelled. What if the shadowy movement were Letitia —what in the world would he do? What would he say to her, what would the conversation be like? Or if she saw him first, what would she do? Would she attempt to kill him? He now regretted that he had not prepared himself better, not investigated what paraphernalia he should have to deal with a vampire. Like everyone else, humanity at large, he had heard of the effectiveness of the crucifix and garlic to keep them at bay. What had been so bizarre an hour before in the security of his study now seemed entirely sensible, even rational. He felt cold, as though a great draft were upon him, and he huddled behind a broad monument where he could still see the iron-grated entryway. He wrapped his arms about himself, shivering on the dewy grass.

While he was already on the ground in effect, he was nonetheless startled to be grabbed from behind and suddenly pinned to the earth. Before he could shout, his assailant hissed his name, "Evan!" He was able to gasp the name of his captor, "Logan!"

"What in God's name brings you here?" asked Logan, his voice low against the possibility of disturbing the dead.

"And I might ask the same of you?"

"Well," he said somewhat sheepishly, "I don't like to overlook any possible bets."

"Like spirits, or vampires."

"Yes, even that," said Logan. "I'm not satisfied about the maid. It was a brutal business. An act of desperation, perhaps, yet with an unusual and cunning subtleness."

"Yes, that seems to be the case," replied Evan. "I am not satisfied with the evidence at all, being at this moment the prime suspect in your book."

Logan delayed answering for a few moments, and Evan hoped that he would dismiss the charges on the spot. But Logan chose his words carefully. "As I have said, I don't believe in this supernatural business. The culprit could be someone who lives in a mausoleum and goes about at night in search of victims. It could be something of that sort. Anyway, as I have said, I shall allow the evidence to fall where it may."

"Your search in the cemetery then was not motivated by the superstition that I fear was attached to my own, as well as my reluctance, my refusal, to be accused at some point of a murder I did not commit."

"Evan, I am not saying that I absolutely doubt your word, but in the end you must give me the guilty party."

"Yes," said Evan, "I shall do everything in my power to do exactly that. But you will have to co-operate in this sense; that is, you must not be so dogmatic, so convinced *a priori* of what the parameters of the case are. I am convinced along with Shakespeare that there are things—" He clutched Logan's arm and pointed toward the south wall of the cemetery. There, walking along in the lightening dawn was Bishop Nestor and trotting beside him, the Bishop paying no notice, was a gigantic dog, almost waist high, with a lolling tongue and fiery eyes.

"A wolf," said Logan, "that looks like a wolf."

The strange sights in the graveyard were not as per-plexing as the situation Evan encountered when he re-turned home and found a hysterical Rachel waiting for him.

"Somethin' awful's happened to Miz Beatrice," she told him, sobbing.

The dawn and the day had been most unsatisfactory and uninstructive to Evan. He did his medical duty. Logan was called, but the evidence of the wounds on Beatrice and on her father did not seem to have any particular impact on him. "What kind of evidence is that? I mean, medically, these people may have prob-lems, but you have no evidence on how these marks got there and really what they mean. Just what do you want me to do about it?"

Andrew was sympathetic when Evan went over the

events of the day; he listened attentively, but in the end, had nothing to offer.

"The matter of Bishop Nestor seems odd, perhaps the oddest item of all these things that you say have happened. Did you have an occasion to bring it up, ask him directly or indirectly what it's all about?"

"Yes, though not very skillfully, I fear. I was so startled about Beatrice's condition—she is young, fortunately, and now is resting well—that I came right out with it when the Bishop came by. He seems to float about, and he startles me. Anyway, he said to my question on whether he goes about early in the morning, on some kind of constitutional, that he does indeed often go for long walks in the early hours, when the mind is at its freshest. I assume he communes with the spirits. As he puts it, the spirit and the world of the spirit is his business."

"What about the dog . . . the wolf?"

"This was a bit more difficult to bring into the picture. I told him of my concern for Beatrice and her father, that their attackers could possibly be animals. From that I led into the question of dogs and wolves. He said that he had never noticed anything of that kind, aside from an ordinary stray mongrel or two, on his walks. Nothing recently. No, nothing at all today. But how he could have missed it, I don't know. I have a witness, a reliable witness, that the Bishop and the beast could not have been more than ten feet apart."

"Perhaps in the dark—"

"There could be no mistake."

"Maybe the perspective was odd, that the beast was not really next to the Bishop."

"No matter, I guess," said Evan. "He was cooperative about providing protection against vampires. At least I can talk to him about that subject freely; he doesn't laugh it off or make light of it. Still, he is skeptical that it is possible to hold off a really determined vampire with, say, garlic cloves."

"Surely he has faith in the crucifix."

Evan smiled. "I suppose so." He seemed embarrassed, as though he were a small boy, confident of the powers of the rabbit foot.

"The important thing, though," said Andrew, "is that I take it he is quite convinced that the Brookfields have been in the hands of a vampire?"

"Unless the wounds can be manufactured, as Logan hypothesizes in the two park murders. That's his case against his suspect who is, as you know, in jail. I don't know what else to do. I've gone out and hung garlic about both of their bedrooms. I have a supply and I brought along some for you, if you have faith in its potency. I left it with your cook, Amanda."

"That is most considerate."

"And I have not one but two crucifixes," Evan said, patting his coat pocket and his chest, but he did not display them, as though they were the wounds in the palms and ankles of Christ.

"Like the cowboys in the West . . . ."

"A gun on each hip? Something of the sort. Yet what harm is there if I am wrong, if the attacks are from bats, rats, whatnot? It cannot hurt to have these traditional items of succor about."

"But what of the victims? Don't they have anything to say?"

"I am on my way to call on Beatrice now. She was really in no condition to discuss the matter then. I have the impression, though, that she was simply asleep at the time of the assault, and is not likely to have anything of value to say. Sir William has no recollection of anything at all. He was surprised to learn of his wounds. And he does not at this moment accept the notion that it is anything other than, say, a spider's mark."

"Not so easy to sell the idea of a vampire, I take it," said Andrew.

"No, and one wonders when one is sensible on this subject and when one goes through the fine line that is supposed to be reason."

"A person can believe whatever he wants. Take our perception of Cuba, for example. Conditions of the population are terrible when it suits us, and not worth commenting on when it doesn't. But whatever the objective conditions are, they do not change."

Rachel greeted Evan in the hall, her eyes apprehensive. "Miz Beatrice is still sleepin'," she said.

She came with Evan to her bedroom, where Evan felt Beatrice's pulse and took her temperature. A fever. Not too high, but it had persisted all day. She lay as though she were in a coma, yet Evan did not think that she was really that deeply into herself.

"I think I shall wait on the veranda for awhile," said Evan. "Perhaps she will awake after a bit. I should like to administer the necessary medicine to deal with this fever."

"I'll be here," said Rachel. "Jis call."

The clear sky and the brilliant sunshine had done little to the weather except to make it even hotter, as though someone had added oak chips to the cookstove fire. Evan removed his seersucker jacket and placed it carefully on the chaise longue. He could picture her there, just the previous evening, charming and sparkling and vibrant with life. Now she lay motionless in her room. What in this world had attacked her so cruelly, leaving her weak and wounded? He would force himself of necessity to develop a new hypothesis, for the one that had been loosed in his brain had come to naught. He stood against the railing of the veranda, looking down into the Lockhart's yard, trying to conjure the scene that Beatrice had described. In his hand was an unlighted Virginia cigar. He reached over to pick up his coat and find a match. He struck the match on the underside of the railing. In the twinkling of that light, in the blinking of that single eye, he saw cowering back from the door to Beatrice's room a terrible apparition, a look of hate and rage contorting the otherwise beautiful and familiar features of Letitia Lockhart. She came toward him in a kind of crouching run, as though to throw herself on him. But Evan, who had been contemplating this awful prospect for so long, was able to reach again into his pocket, flash the crucifix, and fasten her on the spot, as though she had been turned into a pillar of salt.

"And so this scene of murder and carnage at last makes sense, in an insane kind of way," said Evan, the cross between him and Letitia, observing the frightful figure in an unnaturally calm way. His words came as though he were simply making observations to himself, which for some reason he desired to articulate.

"Evan," said Letitia. "It has been a long time. I would have made myself known to you before . . . except I didn't know what your reaction would be."

"I would have done then what I am doing now—seeing to it that you do not harm the innocent."

"Beatrice? Listen how she turns in her rest. She is my friend and she wishes to see me."

"She is in mortal danger, thanks to your intercession."

"Me, my intercession? You are not implying, Evan, dear, that my interests are in the slightest unnatural. You know better than that. If you think it is I who am responsible for her fever, you are indeed mistaken. She is the lover of the same Master who took me from Andrew—and from you."

Evan looked at her closely, partly convinced. "Then why do you return to your 'friend,' as you put it?"

"Only to comfort her. And in the hope that somehow there might be an occasion to meet others, especially you, under circumstances that are not frightening, when the realization that I am still myself overcomes the initial fear."

Letitia stood temptingly on the veranda. The moon provided a softness of background and illumination. Evan could not remember her smile more beautiful than it was at this moment, nor her body so sensuous and inviting. He recalled the white taffeta with the purple ribbons. She had worn it last summer. If he let himself, Evan could believe she was still her old self, only more glamorous and dangerously available. She advanced toward him, smiling, her breasts taut and revealed.

"Come," she said, "there is time and we're quite alone."

Evan was a complex of agitation as she came closer and closer. Just as she held out her arms for a languorous embrace, he held the cross between their faces, so close now he could feel the warmth of her breath.

"You must leave now," said Evan, as firmly as his lust-filled voice would allow. "You must promise never to return to this family, which is undergoing an ordeal —from whatever source. Surely there are other places where you or others can seek out your prey."

A look of pain and anger fell across Letitia's face. But in the next instant she was contrite and humble.

"I should not like to think that you now place all the troubles and problems of this world on me."

"The murders in the park, the murder of the maid in Andrew's house. Why not? You seem to be a good possibility."

She sighed and shook her head and perhaps there was a tear on her cheek. "There was evil before and there will be evil afterwards."

"What about Andrew? Surely he knows about—this."

"I should ask him, if I were you, if you want to find out what he is thinking. I should think that a diplomat would find a vampire as a wife most cumbersome, something to be kept from public view, and if possible, forgotten altogether."

"I shall go and ask him now, if you will come with me."

"He is not home," said Letitia.

Evan turned his gaze toward the Lockhart bedroom. "I thought I saw a light a while ago."

Letitia slashed at Evan with great force, throwing him back on the chaise longue, her powerful fingers trying to close on his throat. At this proximity, under this powerful exertion, her breath was fetid and made him want to retch, and the frightful teeth grimaced in his eyes as he struggled to save himself. The crucifix he had been holding had been knocked from his grasp. He could feel it under his back. He clutched a handful of her hair and began to force her back. Pain showed in her eyes. Now he got his other hand on her throat, pushing her farther away. Then he suddenly released her, snatching up the crucifix as she tried to find a better purchase on his throat. Her eyes were wild with fright, like an animal, and she ducked her head low, kicking at him with her pointed shoe. He grabbed at her, catching the taffeta of her dress and tearing away a portion of the sleeve and ribbon. But as he thought he might make good her capture, she suddenly dissolved, quite simply dissolved into a mist and he stood there, empty-handed, save for the fragment of garment, short of breath, and absolutely exhausted.

For Chauncey Dawson, life in jail had not been all bad. He wondered at his wisdom over the last several years of escaping, with all possible ingenuity and stratagems, from three meals a day and a comfortable bed. To think of the trouble he had gone to simply to avoid institutional care. His knowledge of trains had always guaranteed him mobility, and his detective experience had taught him the rudimentary business of using aliases and keeping on the run. These tactics had made him relatively immune from arrest. But as he had grown older, it had become difficult to keep moving. When he at last settled down in Washington, his money was gone, his health impaired, and life along a river was not as colorful as that described by Mark Twain. He had been miserable. In prison now, his forced abstention from the Puerto Rican rum had brought about an unfamiliar feeling of well-being, a feeling that he greeted with suspicion, and attributed instead to the regular regime. The notion of not having to work for a living, like the idle rich, was the most attractive notion that he had seized on since his incarceration.

The cell block was not crowded and Chauncey luxuriated in his own cell. The jailer was not openly hostile, which was about all Chauncey ever asked of the world, and passed along yesterday's newspapers. Chauncey duly noted his own alleged exploit: "Suspect in Park Slayings Held." This was all that he could read without the aid of his magnifying glass, which he now fished from his torn pocket. "The case of the two mysterious murders in the Oak Hill Park in Georgetown appeared to be on the way to solution with the arrest of a suspect, Myron McLeod, of no fixed address. Captain Eric Logan of the Georgetown precinct said that the evidence will soon be presented to the grand jury. In the meantime, McLeod is in the D.C. jail on $10,000 bond." The article went on to recapitulate the circumstances of the two murders, especially of the Woodward girl. It was that which tended to spoil the otherwise holiday atmosphere that hung about the jail as far as Chauncey was concerned. At the end of that vacation there might be an appointment with a rope. There had been no sign of a lawyer to represent his interest, and being destitute, if one did arrive, he was not likely to be the cream of the profession.

Chauncey lay back on the cot and stared at the ceiling. He loosened his belt which tightly circled his great girth and sighed. If he would plead guilty at some point, perhaps he would get off with a life sentence. Maybe that was the thing to do. But just as he was adjusting his psychological mood to that direction, projected on the ceiling was his bottle of Puerto Rican rum, the full, golden quart. The fumes assailed his nostrils and he smiled. He would not after all give up so easily. There was something to live for, some reason to be on the other side of these bars. The same world which would not abide him success, refusing to him that which it granted all others, had no compunction about taking away his freedom. By denying him the opportunity for success, it made him a pawn in whatever game anyone wanted to play. To have been arrested for two murders he knew nothing about, to have evidence presented that he could not effectively refute—

his own word was worth nothing, Chauncey could tell from the pain and disbelief on the face of the judge as he had offered his explanation, which was absolutely true—this showed the ultimate contempt society held for him. He had been judged alone and friendless, a person who was beyond help. They even denied him a fixed place in the world, claiming that his hovel in the warehouse was not a real address. They had in brief found someone they would destroy, someone who would disappear without a protest, without a trace.

Chauncey felt the tears coursing down his fat cheeks, and he wiped them away with the back of his reddened hands. It should not have come to this had McClellan captured Richmond in the Peninsula campaign, routed Lee at Antietam, or been elected President in 1864. Pinkerton had often talked to him about what might have been had their chieftain been a single step more successful. Had Chauncey known that the days of his youth would have been his only happy ones, would they have been all the more happy, or infinitely sadder?

He rolled upright to blow his nose on a filthy handkerchief. His mind tingled with a feeling of alertness; he would not have been surprised if the bars of the cell dissolved and he could walk unmolested out of the jail and into the night. The bars remained firmly in place, however, but as he sat silently in the darkness, the rumble of snores from his fellow sinners rending the air, he thought he saw someone outside the cell, looking in, trying to distinguish the unfortunate occupant. It was not the jailer, nor a guard. The figure was slighter than that. There was a clanging of the cell block and some shouts and invective, as another miscreant was hurled into the arms of justice and society could lower its sheet an inch or two with the improvement in its general security. The noise made the figure disappear, however, and Chauncey concluded it was his myopia. Yet . . . he remembered that he had been promised help . . . by that extraordinary lady. Now, Chauncey was not the kind of person who would scorn help from whatever quarter, but there was something about that lady that had frightened him more than her reassurances had encouraged him.

The great undamaged segment of his brain began to function again, as he let the prospects and possibilities float about, hoping that in this free association, a poker-hot insight would flash the gaps in the electrical connections in that gray and rotting matter. Suppose, for example, that the lady herself were the murderer, and Chauncey's possession of the shoe was the single factor that would puncture her alibi. He came aglow with this notion, except nothing came out of it, and he became dim, staring at the floor.

Nonetheless, now that he had thought of her promise, she at least did not think he was the guilty party. She had made that clear enough, and convinced him that his retention of the shoe would simply place him, wrongly—that must have been her sincere conclusion —in trouble with the law, his own death warrant. It might be worthwhile for him to make an effort to locate that lady and have her come forth to testify. If he could write a fair description and send it off to Schneider, would the good barber go to the trouble to make the search? It would be a close thing whether Schneider would help or deny that anyone of that name had ever worked there, a corollary of the no fixed address.

It was in this brief surge of hope that Chauncey once again felt the sharp edge of despair. Without hope, he had felt much better, having nothing to compare the situation with. Now that it was there he squirmed in agony and in the pity of injustice. He feared for his sanity. At one moment he could quietly celebrate his incarceration as the best of all possible worlds, while in the very next, redemption and rehabilitation, and the golden fleece of his $5,000 reward, all these were in the uppermost and conscious reaches of his spirit. Thus torn, he sought relief in sleep, the one pain-killing, mind-numbing ingredient that no jailer could deny him.

He slept for he know not how long; he roused himself and stumbled to his feet to relieve himself in the stinking slop bucket. He yawned and stretched and ripped off a series of satisfying flatulations, sat back down on the edge of the cot, and rolled back over, like a child's toy. He lay on the bed for what could have been any length of time, and he thought he was asleep. Then the apparition stood before him, the luminous lady, in a kind of haze. He rubbed his myopic eyes, but the vision remained unclear. Now he thought he was awake. It approached him, to verify his existence, to confirm that he was indeed of this inexplicable and mysterious world.

Now he heard the bell-like voice.

"Chauncey Dawson, I have come to help you, as I said I would."

He could not move from the bed, as though a kind of paralysis had entered his body. He was not so much afraid as curious. He marveled at her courage and cleverness in getting past the guards, although to a pretty face, guards were notoriously corruptible.

"I have found the guilty party in the murder of the lovely Woodward girl, and you shall tell the authorities."

136

"Even if I could provide them with such information, why would they believe me? They are satisfied simply to sacrifice me."

"But we are not, are we?"

"No, that is true. I am absolutely innocent."

"Of course you are."

"What is it I must say?"

"The guilty party is Dr. Thomas, who lives next to the Lockharts', a house that you know."

"Yes, indeed. The owner, Mr. Lockhart, was most uncooperative. Is he in some way involved with this doctor, an accomplice or trying to cover up the crime for him? A tormented fellow, that Lockhart."

"No, not at all. You are beside the mark, as is Mr. Lockhart. From the beginning the doctor has taken a morbid interest in those park murders, thereby gaining the confidence of the police. But in the ways of justice, he is now under a cloud himself as a suspect for the murder of an unfortunate maid in Lockhart's home."

"I have not heard of that."

"It is prominent in the newspapers, which I realize —but no matter. We have loose upon the neighborhood a vicious murderer, and when confronted with the evidence of the child's shoe, he will without doubt confess to the whole series of crimes."

"Yes, yes," said Chauncey. "He must be stopped. What am I to do?"

"Listen carefully," said Letitia, pulling her black shawl about her. She had been forced to stop by her little closet in Andrew's house to change her costume after the altercation with Evan. She could waste not a moment more before discrediting him, now that he had refused her sympathy and had demonstrated that the fragile link that once bound them was shattered beyond repair. Had he already gotten in touch with

Captain Logan or would he delay until the morning? "Tell the jailer that you have words for Captain Logan, information that will solve the two park murders and the murder of the maid, as well. That will bring him round."

"Indeed, yes," said Chauncey, now sitting on the edge of his cot, his excitement growing by the second. "Pinkerton himself would rise for such information."

"You are to say that on your way through the alleyway to the back of the garden and into the park, you had occasion to look into the window of Dr. Thomas' study. He had a number of drawers open, as though he were changing and rearranging the contents."

"Yes, I understand," said Chauncey.

"Now it is in the third drawer that the evidence lies. Say that he placed in the drawer several journals, ledgers of sorts, and then on top of them, he placed a shoe, a black shoe that you saw clearly. A black shoe."

"Why didn't I bring this up sooner?"

"Because you were frightened and dispirited when you were arrested, and upset by the unfair charges."

"And that is exactly right."

"I should not wish to have you do anything that is not entirely honest. You are innocent, and justice will be done."

"With this information at hand, Madame, why do you not approach the authorities yourself, directly, so the wrong will be righted and you would be in position to collect the reward yourself? Ah, there! Now what about that?" Chauncey Dawson drew himself up straighter on his cot and jutted forward his massive head. "I should not wish to be in greater difficulty than I already am."

"I have learned the information from an admirer of

Evan's, who is also a friend of mine, and if I were the source of this tale, I would find it to my social disadvantage. As for the money, the reward, I have no use for it."

"I see," said Chauncey. "So if I spin off this yarn as you say, it sounds as if I shall regain my freedom and five thousand dollars to boot."

"That's exactly it," replied Letitia. It had been a difficult day, tiring, and she had no patience with this oaf. But still, she needed him.

"I was always one to look a gift horse in the mouth," said Chauncey, "and that may be the root of my lack of success in the world of dog eat dog."

"Remember, it is the third drawer on the left hand side of the desk as one looks in from the window."

"Very well, I'll call the jailer the first thing in the morning. What day will that be, incidentally? I've lost touch."

"It will be Thursday."

Chauncey noticed that the luminous lady was weaving back and forth, and he became alarmed. If she were discovered near the cell, there would be trouble, and explanations needed that he could not even begin to fabricate. Salvation was on the verge of being lost at the very moment it had arrived. He was struggling to remove his buttocks from the edge of the cot so he could launch himself forward, but before he could do that, she was coming closer. The form came closer until it entered between the bars and came to within a foot of his face. He looked into depths of fear that so far had not touched his imagination. For in this one point of vision, where his eyesight was acute, where he could separate the details of the facial outline and of the eyes and the lips and the teeth—my God, the teeth!—his cry stuck in his throat, as surely as if he were nauseous, and his mouth hung slack. The teeth were of an unnatural evenness and whiteness, bright in the semi-darkness of the cell, except for the two incisors which, from his low perspective, came at him like daggers. There was a fetid smell on her panting breath and then he felt these teeth enter into the folds of fat on his neck. He wanted to shout out, or flail at her with his ham-like arms, but for some reason he could not move. At the same time, he felt her hand on his member, and he felt the life stir as she kneaded him. He hung suspended somewhere in the middle of the universe, turning on a spit of pleasure.

8

The River Barge

Andrew paced about the master bedroom, undecided as to which of his many splendid belongings he would take with him—which intimate treasures he could scarcely be without, as opposed to the less dear possessions that should be shipped later on. Should he place this longer term responsibility in the hands of Mr. Hooker's firm in Alexandria, or should he turn it over to his butler, Fowler? He trusted Fowler, who after all had been in his employ for more than fifteen years. It bothered him that at this crucial date, problems of this kind were still to the front of his mind, unresolved, when he would need all of his energy and resolution for the hard and dangerous work that he knew very well would be his on the morrow. Andrew's mood was somber. In the bright light of Thursday morning the outcome for the success of his venture was dim. Would the police investigation delay one more day, or take more than one day to reach a conclusion? That was now the heart of the matter.

Still in all, as always, Andrew felt himself to be on the side of justice. And in that role, despite whatever misgivings, he was on the road to saving Letitia from the inevitably unfair retribution at the hands of society. From time to time one thought invaded his mind: if he abandoned her altogether, would he not be better off? The answer came back to him like an echo returning to a traveler standing on the lip of the canyon, a blurred and indistinct answer, a phrase of ambiguity, a simple extention of himself. He would do what he thought was best. And according to the chandler, Hooker, the barge with the earth boxes was already in the river.

He folded his grandmother's wedding ring quilt, no, a double wedding ring quilt, into quarters and patted it into the oiled and polished cedar chest. He looked about the room for additional curios, but decided against the books, most of them Letitia's. After all, the books were replaceable. This kind of introspection and puttering had taken almost an hour.

Andrew looked out of the window for an instant, to relieve himself of his incessant worries. But there was Captain Logan on the stoop of the Thomas house, shielding his eyes from the sun. And then Evan himself joined the policeman, and they began to walk along the sidewalk together. Just as he thought they were safely past his stoop, Logan changed his direction and within seconds Andrew heard the doorbell. He would let Amanda or Fowler answer. He was in no frame of mind to consider questions—his nervousness and guilt were like rouge on his features. He had best be unavailable, hide, disappear, until the unwelcome visitors had gone.

Evan's presentation to Captain Logan of the fragments of a dress which he claimed he had torn from the vampire were not in themselves evidence for Logan to make a vampire his number one suspect.

"If you were not a man of science, Evan," Logan had said, "I would not give this alleged evidence any credence whatsoever. How do I know, for example, that you did not pop by Lockhart's house, and fix up the dress? How do I know that is not the case?"

"Because you know I am telling the truth, and the explanation I offer, no matter how abhorrent to your senses and mine as well, fits all the facts. Beyond that, I have witnessed with my own eyes this Un-Dead woman, and the scratches on my arms and throat also bear me witness."

Logan shrugged his shoulders and sighed. Scratches were the easiest thing of all to account for; if anything, they weakened Evan's story, as though he had not been satisfied with the recitation of the evidence but had been forced by his own conscience to manufacture some as well.

"But still, Evan, what about the shoe? I'm not certain of course that it is the shoe of the murdered child, but I assume it is. And it is easy to check. How do you account for this derelict giving me this information not three hours ago, and here I have in my hand the very evidence?"

"How it could have gotten into my desk I do not know. But do you think, Captain, that if I had committed such a murder I would keep about me the kind of evidence that would place me in jeopardy? It would take a psychopath of some sort to do that, and surely you don't believe I am that. No, we must look at the real evidence. We have two patients nearby, the victims of vampires, as I can show you, and you can satisfy yourself as to the puncture marks. And the attack on me, by the woman, by Andrew's former wife, the struggle for my life—the evidence is in hand."

"So what you want, is it, is that we go next door and ask for permission to inspect the closet?"

"Yes, I do. I want you to compare these fragments with the material of the dress."

"Suppose this person was not so accommodating. Suppose she did not leave the damaged dress in the closet?"

Evan's face was grim. "It is worth trying."

Both Evan and Logan were disappointed that Andrew was not at home. He had not been going to his office this week, Evan had noticed, and the assumption was that he was traveling or on vacation. He had said something about going to New York. Fowler had no information, or in any case offered none, which came to the same thing. Fowler assured them that it was perfectly all right to look about the house. The hall closet was their single goal. Evan's hunch had been right; the dress they sought was in the closet. Logan looked over the damaged garment, and then turned his eyes to the murdered maid's cheerless room, and was profoundly moved. He could not credit Evan with the guile to construct such stories, yet considering Evan's personal and emotional involvement with the Lockharts and with Beatrice, he could not foreclose hallucinations, that someone may indeed have worn the dress, and that Evan's tortured mind could have enacted the rest. But Logan was troubled.

"What would you have me do?"

Evan's answer was forthright. "The crypt must be entered and inspected."

"To do that, I would have to obtain a court order."

"Yes, that is as I understand it."

144

Logan cast his eyes downward. He shrugged his shoulders, noncommittally. "I'll have to think about that."

Logan and Evan parted company in the street, each to his appointed task. It was almost noon Thursday, and time for Evan to look in on his patients. Now that he had taken precautions against future attacks, he was reasonably confident that their recovery was assured. There was no reason to alarm others by raising the exact nature of the malady. Still, the fever persisted. It seemed to him that he had read somewhere that the demise of the guilty vampire would release living victims, acolytes so to speak. One way or the other, then, he would save the Brookfields. He wondered whether to bring Bishop Nestor into his confidence. There was no need to warn him for his own protection. His daily paraphernalia seemed to assure his safety. But it might be well to have an additional ally in case of emergency, thought Evan, and so he looked forward to a tête-à-tête with the man of the cloth.

He rang the bell and stood for a good minute or so with no one answering his summons. Finally, he went round to the rear of the house to repeat the procedure. The door hung open, however, and seated in a well-worn rocker was Rachel. Her eyes were wide open, in a kind of shocked disbelief, and she was paler than he had ever seen her. He concluded quickly that she had been sucked of her blood—large purple patches were showing on her throat. She was quite dead.

After the precinct sergeant was apprised that Chauncey's story of the shoe had proven correct, Chauncey was released from the cell where he had been taken for the interview with Captain Logan. Not one word about the luminous lady, of course, simply the agreed upon story. To his surprise, Logan seemed convinced of its accuracy in all respects.

"What about the reward?" called Chauncey.

"In good time," replied the captain. "See me later."

With that Logan was gone, so there was nothing for Chauncey to do but to wander around the area, enjoying the fruits of freedom. It was a pity that he had been released before lunch, because he was hungry. There was nothing worse than the plight of the forgiven criminal, left to fend for himself. He was now his own responsibility, a dreary prospect indeed, in terms of his next meal. Perfect justice would seem to require free meals for those who uphold the rules of society and are their most dedicated practitioners. Instead, the situation was simply reversed. And if he were to take matters into his own hands, stealing his daily sustenances, his punishment would be more room and board, courtesy of the state. Somewhere in those directions lay madness, Chauncey was certain, but such thoughts would all be immediately set aside once he had the reward. Chauncey checked into the precinct every hour on the hour, waiting for Logan to return.

"Have you nothing better to do?" asked the sergeant.

"No. I can think of nothing better or more promising," Chauncey said.

This response only aroused the sergeant. "Now look here, I don't know when he'll be back. Before the day is through, no doubt. He can get in touch with you anytime he wants. Now stay away from here or I'll run you in for loitering!"

This being the situation, Chauncey in his wanderings soon found himself in the park, and helped himself to an empty bench with a clear view of the rear of the gardens of Sir William, Andrew Lockhart, and Evan

Thomas. And to his left was the cast iron fence of the cemetery. He rubbed the wound in the folds of fat on his throat and became pensive. The connection in his mind between the Lockhart house and the crypt was strong; he had seen the woman quite literally go from one to the other. But how she had then traversed the distance from there to the city jail and into his very cell was the mystery. There was something extraordinary about the whole business. He thought of the bittersweet joy she had brought to him, the curious mark of her affection that remained on his throat. It was painful, but if she had not left her bite on him, he would not have believed that she had actually been with him, that her presence and her story would have been accounted for better as a dream. He would have greatly preferred that. That it was real disturbed him, in the midst of the hope and fear that he would see those lovely luminous eyes again—and the chalk-white teeth. He shivered in the sun and then, after a while, fell asleep.

And so it was about four o'clock when he started back for the precinct building, his stomach rumbling, his bursts of flatulation silent in protest against this unaccustomed fasting. Just as he was passing the familiar trinity of houses, out stepped Captain Logan from the door onto the stoop of the Lockhart house, frowning. He was introspective and did not notice Chauncey. This gave Chauncey the opportunity to station himself at the foot of the steps and to intercept Logan in mid-stride.

"Good afternoon, Captain," he said politely, touching his bowler.

"And the same to you, Dawson," said Logan, stopped in his tracks, annoyed and confused. "Come by the precinct house tomorrow, sometime in the afternoon."

"But I'm desperate, destitute, Captain. I need the reward money now. Surely the Woodward's. . . ."

"All right, then, there'll be no reward."

"No reward!?"

"No, at least not yet—"

"But the shoe, the shoe was found. . . . The doctor—"

"No," said the exasperated Logan, "the doctor is innocent."

"But the clue . . . the shoe. . . ."

"What kind of clue is it that leads nowhere?"

"But surely it is of value . . . that was the basis of the reward, a clue leading to the arrest."

"I'll show you the clue, Dawson," said an annoyed Logan, slightly slurring his words. He held up an iron key. "It is the key to a crypt."

"I don't understand," said Chauncey.

"Oh, you don't," said Logan, beginning to laugh in an odd way, a laugh with a touch of hysteria in it, not a proper laugh at all. "Let me tell you this," confided Logan. "The murderer is Lockhart's wife, who has been dead since last year. She is a vampire, and she sucks blood."

"Is that so?" said Chauncey, his eyes wide in disbelief. Still, a part of his mind and experience fell into line with this macabre suggestion. Certain facts in his jumbled brain slowly rearranged themselves.

"Yes, Dawson, that is so, and so there is no reward for you."

"That's not fair. You can't be serious. Besides, how do you arrest a dead woman, a vampire?"

"You don't arrest them, Dawson. You drive a stake through their heart."

"And then you get the reward?"

"Exactly. Come round tomorrow, after the sun is up, and I'll show you some real detective work."

"I don't believe you," said Dawson.

"And I don't blame you," said Logan, regretting that he had just spewed out the very story he had sworn to keep to himself. It was the bourbon that was doing the talking. He did have the court order to open the crypt, but of course he had not mentioned vampires. He had wanted Andrew to understand that as well, that he was simply investigating everything possible to find reliable information. Surprisingly, Andrew had taken the whole thing rather calmly, and had even provided the key. Logan planned to take along one trusted assistant, so that when the investigation came to naught, the circle of embarrassment would be as small as possible. And now out of annoyance and meanness and bourbon and a desire to ridicule, he had told the old vagabond the truth, or at least an approximation of the truth. Logan himself would be the last holdout from the vampire theory. Surely, through the hard work of patient investigation, a sound and obvious explanation would evolve.

"You're making that all up to deny me my just reward," said Chauncey.

"You don't recognize a pearl when you see one," said Logan.

"Perhaps not, but I would recognize five dollars."

"All right, then, for your trouble . . . and help, such as it was."

"Always at your call," replied Chauncey with dignity. "Don't worry. I'm still on the case."

Logan handed over a tiny five-dollar gold piece, good for enough rum to remove Chauncey from the scene for a week and to rub out, like an eraser, the indiscretion of the moment. In part, however, Logan had misjudged his man. The arrival of the $5 had buoyed Chauncey's spirit and his thoughts had turned to rum. But it had also pricked his sense of greed, and as he sat again in his chair outside the squalor of his quarters, and watched the sun set over the river, he sipped his rum very slowly.

There was a cherubic smile on Chauncey's face that had not been there since he was at his mother's knee. He looked at the purpling sky to remember her work-worn face, but the clouds blotted out all the wrinkles and left in his mind a kind of warm feeling, a feeling of love. "All I am and all I shall ever be I owe to my angel Mother." Had Lincoln not struck that phrase, Chauncey might have at that very instant. The two mementos he had of her were both religious, the crucifix which he wore about his neck and a Bible she had received at the age of twelve for perfect Sunday school attendance. Chauncey had never been able to equal that record. But he had cherished it and read in it from time to time, the tiny print exploding into stately phrases with the aid of his magnifying glass. The smile had come about one hour before, when he had walked down to the river bank, pushed his way through some tall weeds and grass, and arched a yellow rainbow of urine out into the river. Except that it caught the gunwales of a barge instead. And on the barge, the end showing under the tarpaulin, was at least one oversized coffin. And even more intriguing, climbing up from the barge onto the bank, not looking back, was Mr. Lockhart. All this had linked itself inside Chauncey's brain, some strands sagging, others taut. But the total effect had been for him to find a suitable piece of wood and set to work whittling with his knife.

As the sun set, Chauncey was content. The bones

of a roast chicken were scattered about his feet. The rum bottle was stoppered, half full. His mind rolled on. The reward was still not beyond his grasp. Not at all. At his feet, among the chicken bones, were large wood shavings, and beside his chair lay a three foot stake with a nicely shaped sharp point.

"I feel a bit better this afternoon," said Beatrice. "Thanks to Dr. Thomas."

"Don't you worry. The fever will pass in a few days," said the Bishop, puffing on his briar. "Your color is better on your cheeks, and I should think you would be about in no time." The Bishop looked away. Evan's prognosis was guarded.

"It was nice of Evan to loan us Sarah today . . . although she seems edgy. I'll be glad when Rachel is back."

"It is just the weather," lied the Bishop, not wishing to disclose Rachel's ugly fate.

Evan had escorted the body to the morgue, but since Captain Logan was not in a hurry for an autopsy, the work had not been completed. As much as Evan regretted the death, he realized that it was proving his case against the counter-superstition that was the root and branch of the Georgetown police. They were still searching for a regular human being, a phantom perhaps, but still something readily classifiable as *homo sapiens*. With the addition of Rachel to the grim list of victims, however, surely there was more than enough evidence for the most skeptical juror; now if he could manage Beatrice and her father through one more night, the problem and fear would be over. He could not believe that the solution to this wave of woes was not about to be discovered; and an end would soon be at hand for these cruel and unnatural forces.

"Yet I have a strange depression, Bishop Nestor, when I think about the past few days, as though the visions in my sickness were the cause instead of the effect of this misfortune."

"That is something that is shared by all mankind. Don't fret about it."

"But these dreams are so vivid and horrid and frightening, and yet, as I have said before, sometimes I find myself enjoying the spectacle, as though I were a voyeur from afar, watching strange developments."

"You must talk to Evan about them, quite frankly."

"Oh, my, no. I should be too embarrassed."

"I see. But they may give him valuable information in terms of treating your illness, or future cases of a similar nature that he may come across in his professional duties."

"I think my visions, my hysteria if you will, are unique and an experience that should be put aside and forgotten."

"The vision is of . . . bats, did I hear you say?"

"Yes, I told both you and Evan about the bats. But there is more to it than that. The bats seemed to change into various shapes and become—people."

"Real people, or imaginary people?"

Beatrice paused. "For the most part, imaginary. That is, faces of friends who are not here seem to float by."

"A hallucination of that kind is not really unusual."

"No, I should suppose not. But what about the bites —and the loss of blood?" Beatrice blushed with embarrassment, a sign the Bishop took to be one of bounding recovery. But it drained away again, leaving the dry, feverish pallor.

"The wound on your throat seems to be healing nicely," said the Bishop. He knew nothing of the other wound, which Evan feared was not healing. It seemed to have been reopened.

"Yes, I have looked it over carefully in the mirror. But let us suppose that these attacks are simply a kind of virulent bat. Why would it attack some and not others, and why do some recover quickly, and others linger on slowly?"

"It is the nature of today's scientific man to ask why, and then address himself only to matters or problems that are obvious and soluble. And so, in fact, instead of reducing the real area of uncertainty, they have simply made greater the mysteries surrounding my part of the world—that part which has at its roots spiritual beginnings, and such matters as good against evil—into that part of the world these rational men do not venture. But there is where the puzzles lie."

"Very well. Suppose I were to say that on more than one night I saw a dark shadow come toward me, perhaps a bat, which then materialized and took my blood . . . and someone, who is dead, come in the same manner, in a mist, and for the same purpose."

"That would not surprise me in the least—nor Evan."

"Evan! Do you mean he really believes in such things?"

"You will notice the garlic cloves and the crucifixes about your room, the devices from ancient times that have warded off these creatures. They are there at his doing and for your safety."

Beatrice was pensive. "Still, one does not talk about such things. They must spring from the imagination. They can't be real."

"I'm surprised to hear you say that. Yet whether they are real or imagined is not as important as the fact that they influence people and events. To your earlier question, why are some attacked and not others, I should judge that there are those who are mentally and psychologically receptive to such events, and they experience them, while others are not, and do not."

"And is it possible, Bishop, that there are people who long for such unusual happenings, and in effect invite them, even though they may suffer the effect of such a desire?"

"I think that is true, especially in the case of vampirism, for that end is what so many devoutly wish, that is, a kind of immortality."

Beatrice shuddered. "I haven't worried about growing old, but I do not deny that a perpetual state of youth is not an unattractive prospect."

"Vampirism is a problem for the theologians. Like so many things on Earth, it is the degree of good or evil that is crucial. If vampirism were altogether good or altogether evil, it would not be on this earth, but instead, would be in Heaven or Hell. And so the case must always be judged on its own merits."

"You are a most unusual man of religion," said Beatrice.

"My tolerance, my relativism? Oh, I don't really think so, for otherwise I should remove myself too far from mankind and would lose touch."

"I thank you for cheering me up."

"It has been my pleasure. I shall pull your curtains against the coming evening."

"And how is Father?"

"He is coming round. Dr. Thomas will be by later, I expect, and you can learn more from him."

Beatrice felt her fever rise. She was feeble and worn. Her only sadness lay in not seeing her new friends of the night. The night noises were very vivid to her now, and she wondered if she would again see the lustrous eyes of Letitia, and if she did, would she rise to draw wide the curtain, or cower in the bed, the crucifix firm between her trembling breasts? Such decisions, she knew, were in the hands of God.

Thursday evening was coming on and Letitia felt the strength of the dusk begin to flow through her body, as though it were an electric current. One more night and then on the morrow they would be off. What would the day bring? She was bursting with excitement and apprehension. Was there some way to see into the future, find out the answer to a problem denied to people on this earth? She recalled the shadowy Manfred and his demand to his Nemesis to call up the dead—

"My question is for them."

Whereupon the Nemesis did his bidding.

> Shadow! or Spirit!
>   Whatever thou art,
> Which still doth inherit
>   The whole or part
> Of the form of thy birth,
>   Of the mold of thy clay
> Which returned to the earth,
>   Re-appear to the day!
> Bear what thou borest,
>   The heart and the form,
> And the aspect thou worest
>   Redeem from the worm.
> Appear!—Appear!—Appear!

But even the spirit refused to answer, and Manfred was left in the darkness of his own despair.

Perhaps it would be best if she kept her curiosity

in check, Letitia thought. What if the answer was something she did not wish to hear? Manfred might have been grateful too, after all.

She would go to Andrew fairly late in the evening, depending on how her various plans proceeded. She had avoided him Wednesday altogether. By now he would be in a more forgiving mood, and relieved that the murderer had after all been Evan! She smiled at this. She was pleased with her own cleverness, her ability to rectify error and to assure that the quality of justice was not debased. Objectively, Evan had no business intruding in her life, and if he hadn't done so, he could have gone about his own affairs and she would have thought of some other deserving victim. Her relationship with Beatrice had nothing to do with him. By his actions he had become her mortal enemy; she knew, too, that he would destroy her if he could. Time and her own cleverness would aid her, and with Andrew's love, Letitia knew she was indomitable.

The blood lust was already fiercely upon her, as though she had not eaten for days. She had noticed, at first to her regret, that she required more and more blood to maintain her strength. But now she greeted that need with joy. The prospect of the hunt no longer frightened her. It was the source of great pleasure, while the combination of blood and sex was the purest. Once out of the coffin, she replaced the marble slab and looked about. She would not be sad to leave this place. She planned to have her earth box moved directly into the cellar of their new home so that she would be near Andrew, and when he was finally converted, the two of them could rest side by side. She would decorate the room attractively, first for her own pleasure and second, against the possibility of the curious. In the crypt she had never left exposed any of her few belongings—a comb, for example, and mementos from the past, souvenirs of ones she had held dear, little items of memorial, like a belt buckle, a letter opener. She had placed such things inside at the foot of the coffin, out of the way and out of sight. The austerity of the crypt filled her with melancholy.

Once outside, she decided that she must attend to her own need for nourishment. She was alert. There might be some unwary soul still in the cemetery, and perhaps she could come upon the victim quietly and successfully. She had become a mighty hunter.

But there was no one. She clutched her black shawl about her thin, gray dress and started resolutely down R Street. A beggar! He thrust his thin face up to her and held out his hand.

"Ten cents, lady, just ten cents."

"Certainly, my good man. I may even have something more for you."

He followed her, puzzled, but with a growing anticipation as she turned into the alley and smiled at him. Suddenly the possibility of sex and stealing a purse within a short time span filled the beggar's face with a lusty grin.

"Come closer, sir, still closer," said Letitia in her bell-like voice.

The beggar held out his arms to embrace her, and as he did he gave a low cry and his eyes rolled back in terror. Her teeth cut into his scrawny throat and she feed greedily and quietly with practiced ease. He hung from her as though drugged. When she had finished, drank completely to repletion, she let him drop to the bricks of the alley, where he lay whimpering quietly. It had been so quick and simple. She had been titillated to watch the change of her victim's expression, from one of lust and greed over the prospect of what he thought lay ahead. Had it not been in fact for her counterattack, he would have indeed violated her slender body and stolen her purse. She had done to him what he would have done to her, in effect, if he had succeeded. Instead, he had lost. There had been his look of puzzlement, of befuddlement, the inhalation of breath, the wild rolling of the eyes, and then submission, complete submission to her will and desire.

On the opposte side of the street, she looked across at Sir William's house. There were no police posted outside. Perhaps there were some inside, although the garlic and crucifix were probably their alternative. Should she say goodbye to Beatrice, and if so, in what way? Their brief relationship had been unusual in her experience. How sad that they had not met under other circumstances, although had that been the case, who is to say whether it would have led to such depths of love and understanding. Evan would be there, perhaps, but he was not invincible. That he had foiled her assault had been for him a lucky circumstance.

It was Andrew, however, that was her first concern. What would be his mood? Surely he would want to love her tonight, knowing of the dangers of the trip and their separation on the ship. It would probably be too hazardous to move about on the ship. "Stowaway!" she could almost hear the cry. Oh, to be again under proper circumstances, so that she could live a full life! Being alive was one thing, she recognized, but really living was something altogether different. She would join the moonlight and surprise him, at the proper moment.

Logan was seated in his chair at precinct headquarters. The autopsy report on Rachel told the same

terrible tale. The blood was gone from the body, as
surely as if the wrists had been cut in a warm bath.
It was late Thursday night. He was very tired. He
slumped behind his plain oak desk, the unshaded light
bulb hanging down over it, casting his shadow behind
him, so that from afar he appeared as gross as Chauncey Dawson. Aside from the autopsy report there was
on his desk a pint of bourbon, half gone, and a telephone, an upright instrument that connected him with
the other precincts. Behind him on the wall was another phone, a city phone, which worked if one wrung
the crank furiously enough to summon the operator.
He was in touch with his world in a theoretical sense,
but he had lost touch with himself.

His trusted assistant, one Timothy Cleary, had investigated the last murder, and had made his report.
Patterns of activity were not Cleary's strongest suit,
and the finished document had not held the terror
for him that it did for his chief. Logan did not have
the heart to forward it to the superintendent at this
juncture; rather, he would wait until morning. More
likely until noon.

He tipped back the bourbon again, a habit he refused to forego despite his wife Minerva's temperance
lectures, more frequent of late. "You remember your
late father, Eric, and leave the stuff alone." The only
remaining memories of his father were all pleasant,
and he was certain in his own case that if he had to
give something up, he would be wiser to give up
Minerva. His felt hat was soaked where the hat and
head met, and perspiration glistened on his cheeks,
freed by the fires of the bourbon in his belly. His bow
tie sagged in the heat, yet he still preserved a neat
if not natty appearance because of his new brown
wool suit which held its crease remarkably in Wash-

ington's weather. He had decided to proceed with the opening of the crypt, but with great discretion.

"Cleary, tomorrow morning I am taking you with me on a sensitive assignment. We are to open a tomb, an above-ground burial place, a crypt."

"Are we looking for a dead body?" asked Cleary.

"Right you are, Cleary. What better spot to search out a dead body than in a crypt?!" and Logan had burst into wild and hysterical laughter.

Cleary grinned from ear to ear, rarely having experienced such a reaction to his forays into levity.

"I have the court order, of course, but we need to keep a sharp eye about." Cleary nodded his understanding. "And we'll leave from headquarters here at nine sharp. Don't be late."

"No, sir, I'll be here. Do I need to bring—any special equipment?"

"Just yourself, your service revolver, as a matter of uniform, and a torch."

"Certainly."

"And keep it to yourself."

"Yes, sir."

Logan pushed himself back on the two rear legs of the chair and reviewed his earlier conversation with Andrew Lockhart. Calm, collected, no protest at all about his entering the tomb. "Do you want me to accompany you?" he had asked matter-of-factly. "No, that won't be necessary, Mr. Lockhart. I would rather spare you the pain."

Lockhart seemed neither relieved nor distressed. He had proferred the key and then shown Logan to the door with just the proper courtesy, so that Logan felt neither offended nor flattered. Such evenhandedness, Logan thought, could only be accomplished by someone at the height of concentration: not for the first time, Logan concluded that Andrew Lockhart was a driven man. He remembered how the veins stood out on his hands, the hair a kind of bristle, and he remembered the tightness of his smile caused by a certain tenseness of the upper lip. Lockhart had gone through a great deal, of course, having his maid murdered and the only suspect a friend and neighbor, Evan Thomas. Of course Lockhart didn't know about Dr. Thomas' laying the murder at the feet of Lockhart's dead wife. That would make him more tense, Logan thought. At the time, Logan had considered pressing Lockhart for more information about his wife, but it was hard to bring up the question. All he could think of was, "Do you think your wife is a vampire?" which was surely not the right tack. Lockhart, after all, was an officer of the Department of State and could not be treated highhandedly. Besides, this was a delicate matter. He wasn't ever sure he wanted Lockhart to know he, Logan, placed any credence whatsoever in this vampire business. Part of Logan's willingness to go ahead with Dr. Thomas' suggestion was his growing belief that somehow the crypt did figure into the case, vampires or no vampires. The opening of the crypt in the morning might reveal any number of surprises, whatever they might be.

But Logan was not willing to leave Lockhart out of the picture altogether. The canvas of the murders was wide and, for that reason, the details were incomplete. The broad-stroke nature of the case in a way played into his hands, for he was not at all satisfied. As a matter of routine he kept close to his tight little net of river informants, the carp fishermen that Chauncey Dawson had met and spotted. The warehouse area was no stranger to crime. He opened the single drawer in the top of his desk, and reread the note he had been given. "There is a small barge fastened to the bank in front of the rum warehouse," one of his men had reported. "There is a large box on it, perhaps two boxes, under a tarpaulin. It has been here since Wednesday morning. It seems harmless. Still, it is in a position to receive barrels of rum, if some plan of that nature is afoot. The barge is the property of Hooker and Son, Chandlers, Alexandria." The check Thursday morning revealed that Lockhart had hired the barge through Friday. Surely Lockhart was not dealing in stolen rum, so what did he want the barge for? Logan had sent word to the informant to report anything unusual by telephone; that way he could send help quickly, but for what? After the visit to the crypt, he might stroll down to Key Bridge and observe things from there.

9

The Wolf's Cry

It was after midnight when Letitia arrived at Andrew's bedroom. She had given up trying to reach Beatrice again, since the determined Evan and the Bishop were both seated outside Beatrice's bedroom and the paraphernalia noxious to vampires was all over the place. How sad it was not to be able to say farewell! Beatrice was sleeping peacefully in her bed, pale and feverish. Was it possible that she had contracted the fatal fever, from the visits of the Master, and would join Letitia later? It was an exciting thought, yet at the same time, she was not certain that she wanted that sort of competitive situation with Andrew. No, if Beatrice were to become a vampire, she could make her way about Washington or London. Surely she would be sent with solemnity to her native place, where she could reveal her nature at her own convenience. Still, she would miss her. The pace of her breathing accelerated as Letitia looked from this distance toward those cupid lips. But this was no more than a flirtation and without further delay, she joined Andrew.

Except that Andrew was not there. The bedroom was untidy. The papers of Andrew's calculations were scattered about the floor, as though a tornado had cleared the desk. She sat moodily in his desk chair. Her spirits continued to fall with the certainty that this was her last day on earth. Yet she refused to think about this prospect and grew impatient for Andrew. Where was he? She found it difficult to wait much longer so displeased was she with her own company. Then he appeared as though responsive to her wish.

"Darling, what is the matter?" He could see her tears, though she had put her hands to her cheeks to wipe them away.

Letitia cried, her shoulders shaking. "I don't think I can go through with it. You go on and leave me and the misfortunes I've caused you behind. It doesn't matter what becomes of me. Don't link your fate to mine. I'll go my own way. I don't think I want to live like this any longer."

"Letitia, I understand your feeling. I know you are distressed and discouraged. That is why we are leaving for a new place, and finally a new life. I shall be with you as an immortal, like yourself, as I have agreed. Yes, you and I together. You have to hold on for just a while longer, and then everything will be all right."

"Oh, how can it be all right?" asked Letitia, still sobbing. "It is all right, always, when I am with you. But I can see myself at other times and I don't like what I see."

"Together, we will discover a new way of looking

at the world. Just as man has dominion over all the animals, so the vampire has dominion over everything. Do people weep when they eat chicken, or cattle? You must look at the world the way it is."

"Perhaps, in time, I shall. Do you think it will be easier for me after more time? Is that what my problem is?"

"Time cures all things. . . ."

"Yes, a new morality altogether. That's what we will have, Andrew. I don't want to be burdened by the conventions of this age one day longer!"

"Your determination to leave—shall I say escape?—will be sharpened by the knowledge of a call this afternoon, from Captain Logan of the Georgetown police. He has an order from the court to open the crypt and to inspect your coffin."

"Barbarous!"

"It was all I could do to maintain my temper."

"But what about tomorrow. Suppose he comes at dawn?"

"There is no reason to think he will want to get off to such an ambitious start. I assure you that you'll be gone before he comes."

"But why does he suspect *me?* That's so unfair."

"Evan brought Logan to our house, and Fowler let them in. I avoided their visit completely, preferring that Fowler show them around. I did not expect them to find anything. But in your closet, the one downstairs across from the maid's room, they found a torn dress . . ."

"In that closet?"

"Yes. Did Evan tear your dress?"

"It must have been a scrap left in the bushes from my comings and goings."

"In any case, Evan has planted the seed of an

extraordinary happening in Logan's mind, even against Logan's will. But in the absence of better explanations, I suppose Logan will have to investigate the crypt. His heart is not in it, however. He's afraid of looking foolish to his superiors. So he may delay, or in some way do less than Evan is demanding."

"Suppose I go directly to the new earth box now, and not risk another night in the crypt?"

"I'm worried that the barge is under surveillance."

"Then how will it be safe tomorrow?"

"Because it fits into my plan—a plan I have worked out to perfection. All is well, darling. I know what I say. Together we will control our own destinies."

"I hope it has been worth all this danger and despair. Was ever man so generous?"

"Did anyone ever have a better reason for being selfless?"

Letitia was in his arms, covering his face with warm, moist kisses.

"Tell me more, Andrew. What do I do?"

"It's all very simple. Once you feel the darkness, come without delay to the river, just below Key Bridge. We leave from there. Don't worry about Logan. If necessary, he will be kept busy elsewhere with other things."

"But why can't you tell me more? I don't see why you need to be so secretive."

Andrew stepped back and looked at her with pleasure, but shook his head.

"No, it is a secret which has stood me in good stead before, and it shall again. You'll soon know all there is to know about it, and in its simplicity lies its success."

"Your secret will save us?"

"Absolutely."

Letitia suddenly began to feel happier and her somberness began to vanish into the darkness. "It is a lovely night. Shall we go to the garden?"

"Yes," said Andrew, "there is no more need to worry. We are already free. Our life is now our own."

They entered the garden and stopped by the azaleas, deep in the shadow. There was no one visible on the veranda of the Brookfield house, and both of them stared at it for a time. The silence was heavy as they both sealed themselves into their own thoughts.

"The stars are as bright as I can remember," said Letitia at length.

Andrew put his arm around her and held her close. They stood there for a few minutes enjoying the wondrous spell. Letitia asked at last, "What about our personal belongings and all our household effects? What will happen to them?"

"That's more complicated than it should be. Obviously we cannot send them to our New York home, or everyone would be able to follow us . . . although they won't follow us unless there is a specific reason to do so."

"I am not guilty of any murders, if that is what you are concerned about."

Andrew was content to deal that glancing blow, to let her know that he was worried but that once he had her out—chief suspect or not—he would not bring up the subject again. And it was this mutual and unspoken understanding which prevented Letitia from becoming angry at Andrew's suggestion.

"At the second place we go, we can assume new identities and from there reclaim all our possessions. For the time being, I told Evan I'm going to New York on a visit and that seemed to satisfy him."

"Then we can't take much."

"No, darling. Just the essentials."

"I will especially miss my father's books," Letitia said. And she went on, dreamily. "Freed of the fears that surround me here, I will once again pursue my studies, and in time without limit, I shall become the world's most renowned poetess!"

She thought of the lives of Byron and Shelley, so short and bittersweet, Byron dead of the fever in Greece at thirty-five, and Shelley drowned off the Italian coast at the age of twenty-eight. Was it possible that their genius lay in their intensity, a foreknowledge perhaps that their flame was as short as it was bright, and hence the reckless passion for creativity? Without the pressure and presence of fleeting time, would either one have left such a rich heritage? She suddenly began to cry, convulsively, as though she had been the victim of a new, terrible tragedy.

"What is it?" asked Andrew in alarm.

"I shall never be the world's greatest poetess."

"Why not? There is nothing to stand in your way," said Andrew encouragingly. "The genius of poetry lies in your family. I have no doubt whatsoever that you will make that seed flower."

They walked from the garden back into the house. The servants were asleep. They went arm and arm into the hall, past the maid's former room, and quietly to the bedroom. The clock chimed five.

"What I touch tends to wither," said Letitia, "with the exception of you, Andrew. You are the permanent and strong and enduring thing in my life."

"But now you must be off, darling. Spirits up! Everything will soon be happily resolved."

She clung to him again, her mood changing recklessly, like the wind. "Surely there is enough time?" She entwined her arms again about his neck; he did not resist her savage kiss. She could not remember a more satisfying kiss. Or could she? Her mind wandered despite herself. Perhaps Andrew sensed this, or else he was simply distracted by the next day's responsibility.

"You must hurry and rest," he said. "Remember to rise at the first sign of darkness and hasten to the river. Then just do as I say."

"Yes, Andrew," said Letitia. "I am yours."

Andrew smiled and playfully pinched her bottom as he opened the door and sped her along the hall to the stairs. She fairly flew down the stairs into the drawing room. The moonlight added subtle shadows and areas of light. She slowed at the rear terrace door, alert to a new pattern of shadows on the flagstones. Perhaps she had been mistaken. No, there on the terrace was a wolf. It was padding back and forth, sniffing continually, pausing to listen closely, then sitting on its haunches, raising its shaggy head toward the moon as if to howl, but uttering nothing. The Master! She could sense him. She knew she was in contact with the primeval force, going back toward the origin of human beings. She was caught up in her new instinct, and for a time her mind grew blank, as though all the crevices in her brain were somehow obliterated and her mind was nothing more or less than a sponge from the bottom of a tropical lagoon. But this sensation did not last long, and she popped to the surface of reality, as though she had dived into a deep pool and had been spirited up by the natural forces in the pool and inside herself. She was convinced that he had somehow learned that she was leaving, that his prize pupil, who had been faithful to his teaching in all things but one, was defying him and going away without his permission. She had resisted, as best she could, his sexual demands, leaving him unsatisfied.

And now he would completely have his way, by force, as one would break a colt. He waited outside in the shadows. With one bound he would be upon her and ravage her. She could of course transform herself into a bat or a stream of beams that would float through the feeble moonlight, but because of his greater powers, she could not escape that way either. What would happen to her if he overwhelmed her in one of those other modes she had no idea. Still, she would have to try something in order to find refuge against the sun before it was too late.

At first, she thought of going quickly to Andrew to enlist his assistance, but what help would he be against the monster wolf? He would be as vulnerable as any mortal to his terrible jaws, fangs and claws. And the presence of the dreadful vampire, the living terrifying evidence, could again stimulate his resistance to the whole notion of their new life, fearful that in the happy progression that she had so confidently forecast, there would be this evidence that the process was not benign, that those under its spell simply followed their inevitable and despicable course to a hell all their own, far worse than anything dreamed by Dante, and with no prospect whatsoever of a real paradise, save by the most excruciating measures.

Letitia would have to face him alone. Could she escape? She could consider either the side door into the alley-like passageway, or open the back door at the other side of the house. Either way would avoid the direct confrontation on the mottled terrace, but she feared that his sense of smell and hearing had already doomed her plan. Worse, she had the uncanny feeling that the Master was privy to her every thought, that no matter how ingenious was her scheme, she would easily be foiled. And there was so little time.

The sky to the east was now a murky gray; the birds were fitful. Soon the cock would crow and the hundred steps through the garden to the park, and the additional hundred yards to the crypt in the cemetery would be difficult. The moon now fled the field of night and was opaque in the lovely room, and it seemed already darker inside than out. The pale beams on the terrace still outlined the shadow of the restless wolf, pacing silently back and forth. His great head hung down from his powerful shoulders, and it seemed that he too was judging the light. How great a risk would he take with his own existence to exact one final satisfaction from the uncooperative and unwilling Letitia? She stood quietly, tensely by the piano, feeling with her hand the cool smooth finish, the smell of orange peel that oiled so well and faithfully its walnut shell. Her resolution wavered, like a candle flame in the wind. And so with that vision fresh in her mind, she decided. She would leave by the side door, as silently as a mist, but not disturbing the harmonics of the atmosphere by trying to transform herself into light or a bat. She felt her psychic energy approach a low ebb, and she knew that for her, those possibilities were no longer within her power. How much longer could the Master, in the guise of a wolf, maintain his vigil; at what point would he too have to seek the safety of the all-encompassing soil?

She crept toward the side door, facing west, toward Evan's house, like a guilty child. If she could not reach the crypt, she was lost. She stayed on the grass to the west, away from the terrace, and made stealthy progress through the azaleas and lilacs. The wind was almost from the south, giving no indication of her presence to the quivering nostrils of the wolf. She could, however, hear his impatience, as he paced back and forth, and she could hear his low guttural moans.

Letitia knew the path from the house to the tomb intimately. Who in this world had so often walked its way? She was familiar with every root and vine, the languorous limbs of the forsythia that festooned the way, the willows by the tiny pond, and finally the dark foreboding rows of pines that led the traveler to the grandeur of the familiar scene—it all filled her with happiness, as though she were a Roman vestal, approaching a temple in the woods, prepared to sacrifice herself to the Roman night. But these happy and innocent thoughts were as short-lived as the illumination of a single lightning bug.

She could hear the wolf coming down the dark and narrow path. He was still at least fifty yards distant, just entering the gloom of the park. The eastern sky was becoming pink with the assault of the sun, about to burn away the stubborn obstacles to its rightful passage. She felt weak and faint and clung to the darkest shadows as she moved along at a faltering pace. The panting of her pursuer came on without relief. Her one hope was to reach the crypt, for her strength in the growing light was evaporating like the dew. Yet the wolf came on. He stopped for a moment, and then there arose a howl of desire such as she had never heard before, that hung like an accusation over the park, and which was answered only plaintively by a solitary voice deep in the dark of the cemetery.

She was halfway across the grass, nearing the somber entryway to the crypt, when the wolf broke clear of the brush and fixed his fiery eye upon her. Letitia felt her legs falter, as though they had turned to water. She turned to face this menace, at the same time backing slowly toward the entrance of the family tomb. She raised her eyes to the heavens and to the memory of her forebears, in the hope born of despair that the earth would part and that either she or her tormentor would thereby perish. The wolf came slowly toward her, his long, dark red tongue hanging like a piece of liver from the sharp and glistening teeth of his wet mouth. He moved slowly, however, as though his strength was beginning to fade with the ascent of the sun. He came on, uttering low whines.

Letitia felt the cool of the iron gate on her hand. She knew finally the secret of the lock, how to jimmy it from the outside, but that took a few moments more. Her skill deserted her, however, in the excitement of the occasion and she rattled the iron gate loudly in her frenzy. She would have to risk the transmogrification. She turned quickly to see what had happened to her tormentor, whether the imminence of the dawn had diminished his determination. But no, the wolf was still there, with an expression on his face that was not fathomable to her. He stood faltering before her, torn between lust and the desire for life. His tongue darted back and forth like a reptile's, his red eyes dying in the dawn. He snarled and pawed the earth, but he was clearly the victim of the approaching sun.

He had turned to sulk away, his long tail tight between his legs, like a rejected suitor, when a dark cloud fell into the lightest segment of the sky, like a heavy curtain. In an instant the animal rushed at her, knocking her from the iron gate onto the dampness of the morning grass. Letitia raised her voice in vain from the rough treatment of the darting tongue, struck at the vicious snout, only to have her arm clutched by the bright and savage teeth, to feel the blood dripping down onto her face as she cried out against the animal's assault.

There were no answering calls.

The wolf slowly released his grip, his teeth withdrawing from the hold that had in reality barely broken the skin. Letitia, feeling the twin effects of hysteria and the fatal weakness of the growing light, tried desperately to regain her feet, finally with difficulty finding the support of her hands and knees. But she had fallen into his trap. The animal was upon her. He seized her in almost human affection, his paws cutting into her sides, and with a skill only in part bestowed by nature, took her from behind, once, twice, again and again, until the wolf howled with a frenzy that took him to his climax.

At length he dismounted, leaving Letitia with a strange feeling of delight and desperation. She staggered to her feet and this time grasping the bolt correctly through the grill, she pulled open the gate and fell exhausted upon the dampness of the brick. Unsteadily, she advanced to her coffin, raising the pine lid and lying down, face up. She shuffled the heavy marble into place and settled her body uneasily into the contours of dirt.

Her mind would not rest. Had that been the last act of revenge and humiliation of the Master, or was it an intimation of what she should expect in her new life? Would their escape fail, or would she not be fleeing at all, but simply changing the setting for the outrageous acts of an All-seeing Master? For from the beginning Andrew had been right: it was not possible for them to live simply together, feeding on each other exclusively. From that logic there was only the dark and muddy road toward promiscuity. It was her great concern, as it was Andrew's, and now, willy nilly, she had traveled it alone and in her sorrow lay weeping on the eve of her release. The irony and ambivalence of her experience as a vampire filled her with a glow and remorse of equal measure and left her numb to the joy she had so long anticipated. Yet it was not as though this were some ancient dream, some thought that had passed through her girlish head at an early age, when she was certain that children came by the courtesy of the stork, or that love was exclusive, like a cocoon, that the extraneous forces of the world were forever forbidden to impinge on it.

The whole week had left her disoriented, afraid, and disabused, with the feeling that she had been the child of a singularly unkind fate. It was simply a matter of fleeing from these hideous appendages of her servitude that had reduced her to such terror and humiliation. All this would be gone when Andrew led her, like a child of Israel, from this unhappy land, through the seas of adversity, held back by his pure hand, as they traveled again into the land of Canaan.

To be once again at peace with herself. To lead a normal life in society, without fear, and with the knowledge that it was a world without end—such a reward was finally in view. And for all that there was Andrew, her husband, who had taken on all these responsibilities on her behalf. It was the assurance of that love that made it possible to suffer through the ignominies and to accept the peculiar conditions of vampirism which at times played heavily on her conscience. With these turbulent thoughts dashing about in her mind, like the spray of the river in the roughest rapids, she finally found rest. But only for a moment.

10

The Tongue of the Cat

A faint but repeated scraping sound sent shivers down Letitia's spine. Her mood of anticipation changed to a feeling of fright, which temporarily paralyzed her. She wanted to cry out, but she was immobile, caught in the embrace of the full force of the magical earth that would not release her until the edge of night was fastened to the low horizon to the West. She had no doubt who was there. It had to be Logan. She had only seen him once, but even then she had recognized in him a mortal enemy. It was not as if he were a kind of dedicated ferret, a man who had pledged himself to her destruction. No. Rather, she pictured him as the embodiment of the instinct of a ruthless, regimented society that would destroy anything uncongenial in its midst, much as the gardener pulls up the dreaded dandelion from the lawn. She imagined Logan's nose, arched in disgust, his black eyes aglitter with the prospect of ending his own misery by beginning hers.

Alert, she could hear now the sounds of breathing, as though her assailant was closely investigating the vault before beginning his task.

The sound of the marble being pushed aside, slowly, was amplified inside the coffin. It was not too loud a noise, however, as it was shaken back and forth to give purchase on the marble sides. There was a kind of scuffling sound, a gasping pause in the labor, but at each heave the heavy marble moved. Then silence. What was the noise? The purr of a cat? A cat? More heavy breathing and another thrust of the lid. The purring was more distant, as though the cat hung over the edge of the vault and was about to leap onto the pine coffin. Letitia thought of Midnight. If he had not chosen to sleep in that dark hallway, she would have safely left the house, and the maid would still be alive. The scruffing sound stopped. Letitia assumed the lid had been removed far enough to reveal the coffin. Yes, there was the tapping on the coffin lid, which then was slowly raised. A dim light came in over the side of the coffin and then the lid was finally pushed over on its edge. A lantern had been hooked on the taper, rendering the face above her more difficult to discern. The purring of the cat was louder.

"And so, my mystery caller, my luminous lady of the night, is indeed of the nether world. Here she lies, innocent as the snow."

It was Chauncey Dawson, his hair disheveled, his face black against the lantern, his teeth a yellow glimpse, and his breathing labored—and full of rum. There was nothing Letitia could do but undergo whatever abuse he had in mind.

"You are conspiring with the Devil to rob me of

the reward that you, in effect, gave me. What manner of person is this who has such scruples? Surely there is no crime in killing that which is already dead," said Chauncey. The cat purred louder. "Lovely as you are to view, you are evil. And for what? To maintain yourself a bit longer on this earth, to delay the final reckoning from which no one can escape. You are selfish and vain to interfere in the life of the living."

"But Chauncey Dawson," Letitia would have liked to respond, "you don't understand me. Have I not helped you in a most difficult hour? Listen to my story. My time here was unfairly taken from me, and this is the gift I have received in return. Do not condemn me. I must accept, even create, a new set of principles, a moral code, if you will, so that those who suffer my fate—and they are legion—can still contribute to the society that precariously exists on this troubled earth. Share my secret and protect me from the unjust cruelties and retribution of the wicked and intolerant."

Chauncey continued to look into the coffin and tears began to fill his puffy eyes. There were deep lines in his face, accented by the beams from the lantern, transforming it into a kind of grotesque mask. "That it should fall to me to put the dead to rest is something I would not have ever dreamed of. But how else can I collect my reward? Should I simply wait until Logan does his work, or should I gain what is mine?"

Chauncey backed away from the coffin and the cork of his rum bottle squeaked. There was a gurgling sound and then an appreciative sigh. "Ah, but she is lovely. She has, in a strange way, given me pleasure. She is the only person who has given me love and kindness. And now I'm here to end her earthly stay." He began once again to back away. Letitia could hear him sliding to the floor, and she could picture the great head nodding on his chest as he wrestled with his conscience and temporized with his fears.

If she could only speak and reason with him! She would offer him five thousand dollars and much more to let her be, not to concern himself with affairs beyond his ken. There was something demeaning about facing the end she now anticipated at the hands of this absurd figure, a tangential figure in her life, someone who had crossed into her vision only through the incident of a child's shoe. He was to have been her instrument of salvation, but instead, he had become the instrument of her destruction. She would have preferred the procedures of the police. To be slaughtered by Dawson was a mean and bitter end.

The cat now entered her range of vision. It was Midnight! Midnight placed his two front paws on her forehead and lightly leaped onto her breast. When Chauncey noticed it, he was horrified.

"Away, out, out," he hissed, and the cat bounded out of the coffin with a scratching of claws and a scurrying of feet.

Chauncey rose with difficulty and again his dark face was near the coffin. "Poor child," he said. "Only a person with no compassion could see you in such loveliness and not wish to help in some way. I need the money, don't you understand? And I'm doing you a favor, really I am. You'll be much happier dead."

Letitia could hear him busying himself with implements he had brought, evidently in a bag or satchel. She could hear him methodically placing them on the stone floor; she heard the ring of metal. Into her mind, unbidden, came one of her favorite psalms, and she could see herself on a Sunday in church, standing proudly beside her father, reading responsively with the Minister.

I will lift up mine eyes unto the hills,
From whence cometh my help.
My help cometh from the Lord,
Which made heaven and earth.
He will not suffer thy foot to be moved;
He that keepeth thee will not slumber.
Behold, he that keepeth Israel shall neither
  slumber nor sleep.
The Lord is thy keeper; the Lord is thy shade
  upon thy right hand.
The sun shall not smite thee by day, nor the
  moon by night.
The Lord shall preserve thee from all evil; he
  shall preserve thy soul.
The Lord shall preserve thy going out and thy
  coming in from this time forth.
And even for evermore.

And then the glories of the 23rd Psalm:

The Lord is my shepherd; I shall not want.
He maketh me to lie down in green pastures;
He leadeth me beside the still waters.
He restoreth my soul; he leadeth me in the paths
Of righteousness for his name's sake.
Yea, though I walk through the valley of the
  shadow of death,
I will fear no evil; for thou art with me;
Thy rod and thy staff they comfort me.
Thou preparest a table before me in the presence
Of mine enemies; thou annointest my head with
  oil;
My cup runneth over.
Surely goodness and mercy shall follow me all
  the days

Of my life; and I will dwell in the house of the
Lord for ever.

She awaited the fatal blow. She was as composed
as possible. She was eager for the end. She wondered
if the pain of the stake would be so intense as to
overcome the muteness imposed by the day. She did
not hate Dawson for what he was doing. If Dawson
could not understand her, at least she would understand him. There was in any case no way to escape
this sad end. Nothing but thinking of the Lord and
his promise of salvation. *Therefore if any man be in
Christ, he is a new creature and things are passed
away; behold, all thing are become new.*

Chauncey's face was again visible in the lantern
light. His arms were at his sides, and Letitia could
hear the sound of the stake making patterns on the
marble vault as he gathered his courage, for truly
such a task was not the work for the fainthearted.
Chauncey lifted up his eyes and his lips moved in a
kind of prayer. "Now unto the King eternal, immortal, invisible, the only wise God, be honor and
glory for ever and ever. Amen."

He raised high his left hand, and coming down
through the light of the lantern was a long pointed
stake, several inches in diameter. Dawson positioned
it with a quivering hand, but it pricked the shroud
just below Letitia's left breast. To steady his trembling
hand, Dawson pressed down hard, and there was a
sharp pain as the point found its way under the rib
cage. Letitia felt a small trickle of blood. Then suddenly, Midnight who had seated himself on the vault
above Letitia's head, began to scream in a hideous
fashion. Chauncey dropped the stake. But then the

incident seemed to strengthen his nerves and reassure him in his task.

"Foul woman. With this blow, I shall send your soul flying to wherever it may go, surely to hell, *'in flaming fire taking vengeance on them that know not God, and that obey not the gospel of our Lord Jesus Christ,'* and your flesh shall be the companion of the worms of the earth. No more shall you soil the lives of the living. Now go!"

He stabbed the stake again into Letitia's breast, more fiercely than before, and raised the hammer high in his right hand, blocking the light of the lantern from Letitia's eyes. She could not move a single inch to avoid the descending doom. But then with a noise like a shot, reverberating into the coffin in a deafening fashion, the lantern disintegrated and crashed to the floor. Chauncey screamed and the marble lid of the vault smashed to the floor. Midnight yowled and leaped away, into the darkness. Then for some time—in reality only a few seconds—there was a physical stillness that Letitia could feel. The iron door clanged, and then again, silence. And then rising from the silence, a hum, at first like a distant brook. No, more like an electrical apparatus of some kind. It was Midnight, his head next to Letitia's ear. She could feel the brush of his whiskers, the licking of his rough tongue. Then silence as he stepped across her face and settled on her chest, between her breasts. His tail twitched across her face. And he was heavy, perhaps twelve or fifteen pounds, a large cat who earned his keep by hunting mice. But he also killed birds. How many times had Letitia seen him walk across the terrace, a plump meadow lark, or robin, sometimes a blue jay, in his mouth, the feathers stuck to his cheek and a blob of red where the head had been?

Now the cat turned around, facing her, sitting on her stomach, loosening and tightening his claws into her chest, purring and looking intently into the slits of her eyes, his own yellow eyes afire with curiosity. Letitia tried to move her right hand and arm to shoo him away, but she couldn't move at all.

Midnight licked her eyes carefully and touched her lips with his rough tongue, then he settled down again on her stomach, flexing and unflexing his claws. Then she felt a sensation that was not unpleasant, the licking of the wound under her left breast caused by the stake. But soon it began to pain, for as the rough tongue licked, it slightly expanded the area of abrasion. She could feel the cat fixing its claws into her tender stomach as it settled down for its grisly feast.

Letitia floundered in unconsciousness, helpless before the predatory cat. Calmly and quietly, Midnight proceeded to drink her blood. The pain became intense. He seemed to be sinking into her, like a giant leach. Through her half-opened eyes, the proportions of the cat, half-concealed by her flattened breasts, took on a bizarre aspect, a mountain of black fur, blacker than the darkness of the tomb. From the floor there began a low and agonizing moan. Letitia would have almost gladly welcomed the stake compared to the hurt and pain and humiliation of the cat. There was no sound of movement from Chauncey, however, except for a call for the love of God to help him. How strange it was that even in such circumstances as these, hidden from all but possibly the Maker's eye, people in distress would none the less call for help. What was it in the human mind that in whatever situation, whatever posture, it was still worthy of salvation and why, even among those who professed no belief, did the call go up at the end, and the answer come back: *"But without faith it is impossible to please him; for he that cometh to God must believe that he is, and that he is a rewarder of them that diligently seek him."*

Now the cat had stopped feeding on her blood, and his virulent yellow eyes came up low between Letitia's breasts and looked into the slits of her own eyes. He now stood face to face with her, and with his right paw began to scratch at her left eye, which she succeeded in closing tightly before the tentative swipes. The cat seemed intent on continuing this game for the moment. Perhaps he was full and his curiosity might be directed to the victim on the floor. But no, he returned again to the feeding area, flexing his claws again into her stomach, as he resumed his painful lapping. Who could save her from this plight? All her blood might not be enough for the cat. She began to think of the Master, in an abstract way, that he might save her, and soon her mind was full of vibrations. Then louder and louder, more snatches of untranslatable sound. Then she realized what was happening: night had come.

As she felt her strength returning with the dusk, she flexed her right hand. Satisfied, she executed a lightning grasp, catching Midnight by the throat, the wind leaving in a sucking sound. She sat fully upright in the coffin. After the initial shock, the cat began to scratch with its back feet, in a macabre dance that tangled in her gray cerements; then with both hands she began to squeeze the cat's throat. His tongue hung blood-red from his gaping mouth and the teeth glistened from the smoking flame of the lantern burning on the floor. The cat was remarkably strong and tenacious, and the eyes continued their hateful glare.

Then slowly she began to twist in countervailing

directions, until the eyes began to protrude and the head moved to the right. She tightened her grip now, with her full power, and cleanly she wrung the protesting head from the body. She threw the two parts of the animal into the furthermost reaches of the crypt with a feeling of disgust. Finally, she raised herself from the coffin, and, regaining the cold floor, stood beside Chauncey. The kerosene wick burned feebly, casting shadows of the marble slab, broken asunder, on the ceiling.

"Dawson," Letitia said softly, kneeling down beside him, "can you hear me?"

"Yes," came his weak reply. "I am fairly crushed to death."

Letitia could see that part of the slab had fallen on Dawson, pinning his legs. Fragments had hit him in the face and chest, covering him with blood. "You will be quite all right," she said.

"I am at the door of death," replied Chauncey. Perspiration stood from his brow and his hand was at his chest. His eyes bulged with pain and fright. His breath was short, as though witnessing the rise of Letitia from the coffin was too much for his faltering physical machinery.

She loosened his shirt in a momentary flare of compassion, and also his belt. Clattering to the floor fell his old service revolver. A thin smile crossed her lips, and a cunning known only to the pursued glinted in her eyes. She stood up and fumbled about in the coffin, and then she arrayed the items along the wall by Chauncey. Next, she placed the larger pieces of the marble slab into the vault, including the piece holding Chauncey to the floor. It was not needed, for his legs were clearly broken. Finally, she knelt again by Chauncey and looked deep into his eyes. He blubbered in protest and the tears flooded down his cheeks. She affected a tone of great compassion. "You are in great pain. I wish I could do something to alleviate it."

"I can barely stand it. In the name of God, help me!"

"Just as you helped me?"

He saw the cruel look about the corners of her mouth, and he pawed at his chest for the crucifix. He succeeded in grasping it, but his hand and chest were so covered with gore that the blob he produced had no effect on Letitia. Instead, she cocked the pistol and pressed it against the right temple of Chauncey's perspiring head.

"Please, please, lady! I won't hurt you, I promise. I won't hurt anybody."

She fired the revolver, The bowler jumped from his head, but the sound was remarkably diminished by the closeness of the muzzle to his forehead. There was gore against the marble wall but the forehead simply showed a black seeping hole. She placed the pistol snuggly in his right hand and stood up, admiring her own handiwork.

Mindful of Andrew's exhortation to go quickly to the river upon the onset of darkness, Letitia searched about the crypt for something more appropriate to wear on her departure. Her dress was soiled and spattered with gore. The torn taffeta gown with the purple ribbons was about the only serviceable garment left to her, salvaged before the closet had finally been cleaned out. There was an excitement in the wind. Already she could hear the howling of wolves, as though they were running in a pack. She could hear the chirruping of hundreds of excited bats, low under the clouds, hunting and darting close to the earth, searching for the spot of blood that is an insect.

She looked about the awful scene with more satisfaction than horror. There had been a certain rightness about this settling of debts. Her sadness, though, stemmed from the realization that this was indeed an ending of an important phase of her existence. She could think of those little landmarks from the days of her childhood to this moment; out of each ending there was necessarily a new beginning.

> So we'll go no more a-roving
> So late into the night.
> Though the heart be still as loving
> And the moon be still as bright.
>
> For the sword outwears its sheath
> And the soul wears out the breast,
> And the heart must pause to breathe,
> And love itself have rest.
>
> Though the night was made for loving,
> And the day returns too soon,
> Yet we'll go no more a-roving
> By the light of the moon.

Odd that she should think of that poem. Surely her dream had not already ended before it had even begun. She walked softly down the aisle of the crypt. The kerosene wick had burned itself out. She looked back briefly. The two bright eyes of Midnight glowed like gold buttons, burnished and on fire. Chauncey's bulk was lost in the gloom. At the gate, she transmogrified into a bat, with some difficulty. While it was dark outside, it did not seem dark enough. Something was wrong with the sky.

Bishop Nestor sat is a straight-backed chair, his head bowed, his hand clasped in those of Sir William Brookfield, his eyes closed, his lips moving in a kind of chant, a repetition of some wise words of ages past. The turning to the past for wisdom was a curse of the human race, as Tennyson had remarked, although few had grasped the point he made, a victim of his own eloquence.

The old order changeth, yielding in place to new.
And God fulfills Himself in many ways,
Lest one good custom should corrupt the world.

He could not believe that Sir William was dead, dead absolutely. And the tiny puncture marks on his throat were mute evidence of the malefactor. The Bishop blamed himself for his fund of wisdom that now seemed so naive in the face of death. Tolerance was really what his spiritual mission was all about, yet if it was his virtue, his good custom, it had corrupted him altogether. The golden mean was all he thought possible in this world. This would mean a place that would honor reason, that anything in excess would, by universal sentiment, be banished. The excessively good and the exceessively bad would thereby be ostracized. A little evil was not necessarily bad, for without that yardstick, how would it be possible to judge what was good?

"Old friend," said the Bishop to the stiffening body of Sir William, "what can I do to repair this awful damage? I didn't think the vampire, essentially a frightened fugitive, would drain your blood in excess, causing your death." He looked with pleading eyes at his friend. "I was not vigilant enough. Can you forgive me?"

No answer forthcoming, the Bishop leaned back in the chair. He consulted his watch. It was just eight o'clock on Friday morning. He would have to notify the authorities. Poor Mr. Logan. How this news would offend him! Of course, some strips of plaster judiciously placed would conceal the tiny but deep wounds and simplify the analysis. Sir William was after all not a young man. He had lived, in fact, a good long time. The Bishop could not really date the man. Human beings were not like trees that one could simply saw in two to count the rings. Still, he regretted his death. Compassion. The Bishop knew that he had an excess of compassion for all creatures under Heaven. A harmony of men and nature, the quick and the dead, of all seasons with all growing things—these were his ideals, his fantasies. Yet he had seldom been disappointed before, and the blank face and unhinged jaw of his dead friend now mocked him.

Of course, he might have expired from another cause. The old wounds may simply have become infected. Only the autopsy would tell. Perhaps he was unjustly blaming himself for nothing. He would do his duty to his friend by notifying Logan. He would simply telephone. Then he would leave. He had been here longer than he had intended. He would take up a mission elsewhere. He tried to remember how long he had been in America. Had he come in 1879? Such a long time ago. Suddenly, he felt tired. The battle of good against evil, and evil against good, was a fierce one, without respite. It did not seem to yield to any simplification, any kind of reductionist philosophy. It was all-embracing, all-encompassing. Still, he had no intention of giving up the struggle.

Finally, he rose from the chair and applied the adhesives. Then he lovingly pulled the sheet up over

Sir William's face. Before making the phone call, he would apprise Beatrice of the sad event. She was not too strong herself, but thanks to Dr. Thomas' attention, there had not been a recurrence of the attack on her, as far as he knew. She would be shocked at her father's death, but she was a brave young lady and would rise to the occasion. She would probably return to England and take up residence in the historic building of her father's estate. Or would she remain for a time to see if her romance with the doctor would blossom?

He knocked gently on the door. And then, louder. No response. Finally, and with proper timidity, he entered the room. The bed had been slept in, but there was no evidence of Beatrice. The door to the bath was standing open and the room was empty. He proceeded to the veranda, knowing her pleasure in sitting on the chaise longue and viewing the garden. Still no one. She was gone.

Eric Logan was in a grouchy mood as he and Cleary walked along Q Street on their way to the cemetery. He knew that they would find absolutely nothing to substantiate the notion of a vampire being behind these murders. Was Evan trying to deceive him, send him off on the proverbial wild goose chase, while the guilty party escaped notice? Possibly. But if that was the game, each passing day would make the culprit more assured of his safety, and through the accumulation of little slips, the noose would finally settle around the guilty party. He had seen it happen, time and time again.

"Nice day, Captain," said Cleary, anxious to stir his chief from his private meditations. "I prefer to set about this kind of task in the bright weather. In the rain or fog, or at night, I don't mind saying I get a bit nervous."

"Nothing to get nervous about today," replied Logan. "This is a court formality that must be done. I would have done it by myself, but a witness is required."

"I appreciate your confidence in me," said Cleary.

"You are a reliable fellow, Cleary, and I won't forget it."

Scarcely were they inside the main cemetery gate, however, when the sky suddenly changed. The wind swooshed about them, and the bushes and trees paid it homage. There was an eerie feeling about the darkening sky and the confidence and good humor born of the sun and brightness dissipated.

"What's going on here?" asked Cleary.

"Odd," said Logan, shielding his eyes to a dimming sun. "Why, it may be an eclipse. A solar eclipse."

The penumbra was in fact almost on them, as they came along the side of the crypt. Suddenly, above them, as though hanging in the sky, was a large bat, flying now faster and faster toward the river.

"I forgot the key. Jimmy the door," said Logan.

This accomplished, they stood at the door, looking at each other, the darkness becoming more intense.

"Shall we wait until it's over?" asked Cleary.

"We could, I suppose," said Logan, Cleary's unease reinforcing his own. "But no, hand me the torch. And follow close along." The light began to pick up the marble squares, one by one, until it found a guiding path, in a slowly widening ribbon of blood.

11

The Green Bottle Fly

The light puzzled her. It was not the dimness of the dawn nor the languid purple of the evening. Yet it was dark as she flew up from the crypt and saw the startled face of Logan, looking up in fear, with his slack-jawed lackey by his side, exhibiting even more surprise. She had left not a moment too soon. Andrew's charmed plan was a bit too tight for comfort. And even though she was free, some concern still tugged at her.

What was it? Where was the feeling of jubilation she had expected? There was something yet unreconciled, as in the conversation between Manfred and the Abbott toward the end of the tale, on the prospects of absolving his soul. "It is too late," said Manfred. The Abbott answered, "It can never be so, To reconcile thyself with thy own soul. And thy own soul with Heaven. Hast thou no hope?" And the Abbott continued, " 'Tis strange—even those who do despair above, Yet shape themselves some fantasy on earth, To which frail twig they cling, like drowning men."

Perhaps it was just the fact of leaving Georgetown. It was the familiar place of her youth, and her departure seemed so final and irrevocable, furtive and fleeing, while a proper way to have gone would have been altogether different. Evan would be totally relieved to learn from Logan that she was no longer about and would rejoice. Her departure would quicken his courtship with Beatrice, in the absence of competing forces. She herself had barely known Beatrice, and now even the memory would be poisoned as Evan pressed his own advantage. No, it was far better to stay not a moment longer, to rejoice in Andrew's dedication and forethought to be on their own way, to lead their own happy life. It would not be easy at first, she suspected, but they would persevere. As Andrew had said, as he had written in his diary, he had made his commitment, and that commitment was to love.

Now she could see Andrew at the edge of the river. He was near the empty wagon in which he had brought the belongings they would need in the future, the essential items of the past and of the future. Everything had been transferred to the barge and covered by a tarpaulin. He was moving the horses and the wagon further up the bank now, where the horses could graze on the odd clump of grass. Letitia flew into the line of lofty, leafy maples that ran along that section of the river bank, flitting down to the forsythia bushes and then stepped out in her corporeal form. To her surprise, it was not Andrew but Bishop Nestor who greeted her.

"Andrew has asked me to assist you at this moment.

He has explained the whole situation, so do not be afraid. I want to help. Andrew has to contend with a variety of problems before the two of you can safely proceed down the river." The Bishop spoke like an old friend, and she was grateful for his simple explanation. What more was there to say?

Andrew was now walking up-river toward Key Bridge. From the crest of the ridge nearby, came a gray band, a dozen or so sepulchral forms, who upon seeing Andrew, stopped as though he had held up a symbol or cast a spell. They seemed to freeze on the landscape and become smaller as they sat on the slope at some distance. Andrew raised his hand in a kind of benediction and they were quiet and content. More of their number gradually joined them.

The scene was calm for the moment, but Letitia nonetheless felt a powerful agitation wrack her body and Bishop Nestor, noticing her distress, placed a comforting arm about her shaking shoulders.

The heavens were steadily growing blacker, as though the skies would again thicken and rain. But on the contrary, there was a lightness to the air, even a dryness, which contradicted the possibility of rain.

"What is happening?" asked Letitia, looking up into the sky. Suddenly a single shaft of light, brilliant light, blazed from the edge of the encroaching moon and landed on the far end of the dark horizon.

"This is nothing more or less than a full eclipse of the sun," said the Bishop, "which occurs every 6,585 ⅓ days, or about every eighteen years, in different parts of the world. We are now covered by the umbra, the darkest moment. When the light returns, in about seven minutes, it will once again be day as usual. Like Andrew, I have studied this phenomenon for years, and while it is always exceptional, there is a simple explanation known from ancient times. Do not be frightened, Letitia. Do not look at the sun, for even though it appears dark, it will blind you."

"So Andrew was this farsighted. But once in eighteen years!"

The Bishop nodded. "Clever fellow, Andrew. You see you are already safely here."

"But why didn't Andrew tell me?"

"For your own sake. If you knew, perhaps someone else might have found out that information. And it has other important consequences."

The moon now covered the sun. The wind rose and the dust and leaves swirled along the river and rippled the surface of the waters. The barge was firm against the bank, the tide having reached its height.

Letitia was watching the gathering on the higher part of the bank.

"Who are those strange people?"

"They are not truly strange," said the Bishop. "What you call strangeness comes from their different customs. You see they are Un-Dead from the past, the refugees of time's progression."

"I had no idea there were so many."

"Yes, I fear that the very large number is at the center of the problem. With so many mouths to feed, they at last attract hostile attention, threatening the existence of all vampires."

"Where is the Master? The vampire who is responsible for my condition, for bringing me into this kind of existence?"

The Bishop paused and fingered his hemlock crucifix. "I don't know, but unless he has fallen victim to a stake, he will surely come. I'm certain of that."

"I am afraid both for myself and for Andrew."

"When the moment comes, trust in Andrew."

Letitia followed Andrew's progress up the bank. He climbed unhurriedly as though he knew precisely what he was doing. Then like a golden ball, Beatrice came over the crest by the abutment of the bridge. Evan followed behind her. "Darling!" she called. Andrew seemed confused and looked back at Letitia, and Letitia in turn looked at Andrew. To whom was Beatrice calling?

"Just as I thought!" cried Logan, in a tone of triumph and relief. Above all, the sense of relief, as though a dam were about to be breached by a great flood of gratitude and thanksgiving.

Cleary took a less charitable and grateful view of the ghastly sight on the floor, going immediately and directly to the outside of the crypt where he proceeded for a time with the unpleasant business of being sick, leaving the investigation for the moment entirely in the hands of his superior.

"And so it was like this all along, Dawson. You and you alone operating out of this crypt, where no one would think to look, to take advantage of the dead to kill the living. What a monster! And here is where you stored your bloody souvenirs. Yes, the other shoe, the belt from the housekeeper, Carolyn's letter opener, Rachel's silver bracelet, her single bit of finery. What a demented beast! No wonder that even you could stand it no longer. Even you were forced to blow your brains out, surrounded by the evidence of your misdeeds, knowing that I was coming here. I would have exposed you and brought you to justice. So you took your own life. Or was it the hand of God, who could no longer look upon such ugly, brutal crimes?"

Logan swung the light about the floor, seeing the marble remnants scattered about. He also looked at the ragged ends of marble showing above the vault. He started toward the vault, then stopped, and turned the light back onto Chauncey's bloody bulk, the great head hanging forward on his chest.

"And worst of all among your crimes you raised the spectre of the occult, the unnatural, as the source of this evil. Even I was almost persuaded. It shows, I fear, how very near the surface lies the superstition of the ages. It takes so little to bring it out. It begins with the proposition that if you do not understand an action, a murder, by material and logical evidence, why then it must needs be searched for elsewhere. How convenient, how corrupting."

His eye was attracted to something coiled about Chauncey's neck, caught in the coils of two rolls of fat. He pulled up the rubber hose and the familiar valve. He shook his head again.

"A one man wave of terror. So he made himself another hose to continue his foul work. We arrested the right man in the first instance, but refused to believe the evidence. Remember that, Cleary, if you expect to advance in police work. Remember to believe the evidence. If you do that, you will be right nine times out of ten."

Still, the glory is always in solving the tenth case, the one when the obvious answer is simply wrong. Logan's reverie was interrupted by the sound of marble being dropped, none too gently, on the floor of the crypt.

"What are you doing, Cleary?"

"I thought you wanted to open this coffin. Letitia Lockhart? The business of checking if there was a mistake?"

Logan said nothing, as he struggled with his own curiosity and his duty to the department.

"The court order you got, sir, to check if perhaps—"

"That was a ruse, Cleary. I had to have permission to get in here, and that seemed to be the easiest way."

"I see," said Cleary enthusiastically. "You could have fooled me."

"We found what I was after. I'll report the damage to the vault to Mr. Lockhart, which I do not doubt is the responsibility of this scoundrel on the floor."

"Or of that big bat?"

"Not the bat, Cleary. Already you are ignoring my advice. Look, you go back to the station and get the coroner and have him come over here and clean this up. I'll stay a bit longer and pick up the rest of the evidence. This is the fellow who was responsible for all of the murders, all the trouble we've had this spring, from the park to the maids."

"You don't say. Even the one reported this morning around eight? The British fellow, the diplomat."

"And what makes you think that was a murder, Cleary? Everyone is edgy these days. What makes it so improbable that a man in his seventies passes away in his sleep?"

"Someone said it was murder," said Cleary.

"Best to check those kinds of rumors out very carefully yourself, before going about spreading such things. Bad for the department."

"Yes, sir," said Cleary, the tone of the captain's voice finally making him understand the extent of his error and the desirability of finding the coroner with no further delay.

Logan waited until Cleary was out of sight. Then he went over to the vault. He really didn't want to see if the body was there. If it wasn't, it would only complicate his theory, which was now complete. With great difficulty, he removed the marble chunks and raised the coffin lid.

"Empty!" he said softly.

He looked again at Dawson and the neat row of evidence of the murders, plus the revolver, the suicide weapon, in Dawson's own hand.

"He probably removed the body either for gain by selling it to a laboratory, or simply because of some ghoulish delight. There is no point in saying anything about it." With that he closed the coffin and resettled the heavy marble on top of the lid.

After a few more minutes, Logan went outside of the crypt, having placed the evidence in the pocket of his suit coat. He wrapped the rubber hose around his left wrist and tightened it in place. He leaned against the marble crypt, shading his eyes to the south and east, where the moon clearly held the sun in its grasp. Well, he would concede that sometimes things did go contrary to nature, but in the end, nature always righted itself. He smiled as the first burst of light flickered along the edge of the moon.

As the strange scene unfolded on the slope toward the bridge, Letitia clung to Bishop Nestor, and he patted her head in a gesture of comfort. There was more fluttering of birds and the yipping of dogs. This was not, however, what frightened her. It was the reemergence of the very thinnest edge of the sun from the shadow of the moon.

Beatrice was coming down the bank toward the huddled group. Suddenly she stumbled and fell. She lay still about halfway between Evan, who was now at the crest, and Andrew who halted halfway up the slope. The scene was fixed as though one were viewing a painting, overwhelmed by elongated people, perhaps an El Greco. The sliver of steady light, high on a distant cloud, filled Andrew with alarm, which showed on his face as he turned to look toward the barge. Letitia watched in wonder as he halted his move toward Beatrice. She was again on her feet, breathing heavily, throwing out her arms in a kind of entreaty, but almost unable to move. Her odd gait was a step forward, two or even three side steps, then a backward retreat up the slope. She seemed like a passenger rushing to the gangplank for a pleasure voyage, too late to quite reach the receding vessel, which in this case was Andrew. Andrew was now returning to the barge, like a mountain lion, steady and sure in his step, but ever backward. No one spoke. Each instant seemed like a year, an eternity, for Letitia. She had understood very well the acceleration of time, as though there were no clocks, no arbitrary division of time into days, or weeks, or months, or years. Or milleniums, in the minds of the philosphers. The picture before her eyes moved in a jerky, mechanical way, and the sound of voices came from great distances. Or from very close, as though someone were whispering in her ear.

"Andrew," came the golden voice of Beatrice. "Take me with you! You have promised. Remember, darling, you have promised!"

Andrew held up his hand in a kind of farewell salute, his eyes not focused on Beatrice at all but on the sliver of light that was now growing wider, and was slicing down the cloud to the far end of the bridge. Letitia smiled. Beatrice had been mistaken about her lover. She had assumed that it had been Andrew, when it had been Letitia and the Master all along. Or had Andrew found an opportunity to encourage Beatrice secretly to expect his allegiance? Letitia laughed out loud at the plight of poor Beatrice, now fallen again, delirious, feverish, and the distance between her and Andrew growing wider by the second.

As Andrew withdrew, walking backward down the slope, Bishop Nestor joined him, clasping his arm about Andrew's shoulders.

"There is very little time, Andrew, and you had best make use of it."

Andrew nodded, yet he seemed reluctant to lift his feet, as though he were committed to that very spot of rock and grass on the slope, and that he would fall, like Beatrice, and rest.

The band of light was now sliding swiftly across the bridge. The rim of the sun burned brightly, as a sulphurous gas, as thought the image of hell had been transmitted to the sun, and had in that process, been magnified and intensified. The brightness of the sample of the sun, after the eerie time of darkness, was as the blacksmith's forge.

Letitia found herself becoming more ill at ease, as Andrew and the Bishop continued their quiet conversation, in no hurry to reach the barge, which rocked so gently in the river. Letitia sensed the urgent need to go. The scythe of the sun was cutting down now, coming to the slope where Beatrice lay. Evan was now in the full sun. "Beatrice, darling, I will save you. Do not go on. Stay where you are until I reach you."

Beatrice seemed spurred by his call, but instead of turning toward him, rose and took three more steps into the darkness. Andrew urged her on, but the Bishop tugged Andrew back, speaking in a strange tongue that Letitia could not understand. Letitia moved instinctively toward the barge and the protection of the earth box as the sun's rays came ever closer. She glanced at the sun, at the fading moon, as the eclipse was on the wane. There was something terribly unnatural about this occurrence, as though the moon swallowing the sun were against the proprieties of nature. The calls of the birds and the animals were louder and frantic, to welcome another dawn so shortly after the legitimate one had come but four hours before. This would restore their world to normality, but would it do the same for hers? Who would help her? To whom could she turn?

Andrew now tore himself loose from the Bishop's grasp and raced a dozen steps up the slope, holding out his hand toward Beatrice, who was unable to respond in kind. She seemed to call his name, but it did not come forth from her lips. Instead, there was Evan's call. "No, Beatrice. Look back to me, not to the shade. Look back to life."

At that very instant, the sweep of the sun caught Beatrice on the slope. She gave no alarm, no cry of pain, but she became still and silent, as though she had fainted away. Her blue eyes, however, suddenly turned a dull gray, the way the eye, for example, of the living fish, all black and gold and bright, takes on a dull green and grayish hue at the moment of—death! Evan continued toward her as the sun-belt moved on, ever edging down on the slope and still in slow motion.

Fleeing from the light came the Bishop and Andrew. Andrew was weeping bitterly. "She was late. Why was she late, Bishop? How could this happen?"

The Bishop was slow to speak, but he looked back at Evan, who was holding Beatrice's dead body, rocking her back and forth as tenderly as a child, loud sobs coming at intervals.

And now Letitia looked up toward Evan and farther

to the right where all the Un-Dead lay writhing on the ground, writhing like so many earthworms on a hot griddle in their last agony.

"All is not lost, my son," said the Bishop, "but I implore you to waste no more time. You must take on your responsibilities and be off, forever."

Letitia came quickly from the shadows and held on to Andrew's arm. He seemed startled and preoccupied. He stared in the direction of Beatrice, but then turned and leaped onto the deck of the barge. He removed the tarpaulin and raised the heavy lid of the first earth box.

"Come, Letitia, there is no time to lose!"

She saw three boxes, two dull, gray earth boxes that Andrew said he had imported and the third the great cedar chest from the master bedroom of their home on Q Street. Letitia, however, stood by the Bishop. She made no move to reach the barge. "Andrew, you don't want me any longer. How foolish I was not to understand that your love was no longer for me. That you did not want to have me forever, but instead, had chosen another to take with you on this journey. Had she come, what would have become of me?"

"Letitia, there is no time for argument. I would have taken Beatrice too, that is true, but do not blame me for her condition. It was not I who made her into a vampire. Consult your own heart."

Letitia felt the hot tears of shame run down her face. But she had not certainly brought Beatrice to this terrible state, where her conversion had been so advanced that the bright rays of the sun had left her dead, bloating in the heat? No, she could not have done it by herself.

Bishop Nestor looked on her kindly, but now in a more secular way, pointing to the earth box. "Here, Letitia, you still have an eternity ahead. Hurry. Only a few are immune to the sun." He raised his hemlock crucifix over the open box full of red Virginia soil and it turned to a gray mulch—unconsecrated earth!

But Letitia did not wonder over this miracle. Her mind turned on herself. A lifetime. An eternity. Forever tied to the blood lust, which was already eating away their love for each other. Would it be that way forever? She feared that the pangs of necessity would always outrun the singleness of passion, which she now realized was the supreme human condition, outside the moral precepts of any vampire, no matter how virtuous. She smiled at her self-recognition, her delusions about the purity of her love as she lay with her lips on those of Beatrice, the broader lips of love wherein lay the sweetness and the sorrow. She was suddenly repelled by herself. She felt faint with shame and remorse.

"Hurry, Letitia," called Andrew. Bishop Nestor was already on the barge. Once more, he urged her to come.

Again in the frozen frame of time, she looked from the dark into the light, where Evan was mourning Beatrice. It was so terribly, terribly sad. Letitia thought again of Manfred and the frightful final scene, when the spirits were offering to save him from his approaching death. Manfred spoke: "I do defy–deny–spurn back, and scorn ye!" And the Spirit replied: "But thy many crimes have made thee. . . ." And then Manfred hurled back his response.

What are they to such as thee?
Must crimes be punished but by other crimes,

And greater criminals?—Back to thy hell!
Thou hast no power upon me, that I feel:
Thou never shalt possess me, that I know:
What I have done is done; I hear within
A torture which could nothing gain from thine:
The Mind which is immortal makes itself
Requittal for its good or evil thoughts,—
Is its own origin of ill and end—
And its own place and time; its innate sense,
When stripped of this mortality, derives
No color from the fleeting things without,
But is absorbed in sufferance or in joy.
Born from the knowledge of its own desert.
Thou didst not tempt me, and thou couldst not
    tempt me;
I have not been thy dupe, nor am thy prey—
But was my own destroyer, and will be
My own hereafter,—Back, ye baffled fiends!
The hand of Death is on me—but not yours!

Letitia looked at Andrew, into his cold eyes and
sullen face. He seemed a different person. She would
have to find it in herself to forgive him. Yet her heart
seemed to pulverize, as though a Christmas cardinal
had fallen from a branch of the decorated pine and
shattered on the polished oaken floor. She saw Bishop
Nestor raise his hemlock cross toward the fading
darkness and without a word, perhaps through his
passion for the relativity of all things, simply walk
from the barge, as though going through a door, and
vanish.

Andrew jumped back on the bank, his cloak flowing
about him like an inky pool. He set about casting off
the lines. "Hurry, Letitia." At that instant Letitia felt

the power of the sun on her back and fell heavily among the grass and weeds, part in the sun and part in the shadow. She could feel her spirit struggle feebly within her, as she watched Andrew. Would he now come back and rescue her? Or was he simply leaving her here to die?

"Andrew!" she called softly, as softly as the breeze that now stirred the grass at the edge of the river. He stopped as she called, and slowly began to turn in her direction, still at the maddeningly slow pace that had dominated the scene for the past several minutes. She looked at the grass, and each single blade was an object of wonder and delight, and the new dandelions looked as pretty as buttercups. She reached to pluck one to rub under her chin. The sun became hotter, suddenly, as though it were the blast from the door of a furnace, paralyzing her legs and reaching up toward her heart.

"Andrew," she whispered once again. By now the barge seemed to be shimmering in the water and from the grass it looked as though it were headed out into a gloomy tunnel. Andrew turned toward her. All she could see as her eyes began to cloud over was the black hat, and below it a white face and in that face, two glowing red eyes and a great black square of a mouth, like the maw of a spider. And now finally, she understood, that the Vampire described in Andrew's journal was Andrew himself. The commitment to love he had mentioned was self-love. Andrew had destroyed all the vampires to insure his own continuity. Letitia herself was to be sacrificed.

The perspiration burst from her face like a flood. She heard the buzzing of the bees, and she thought that she saw the dark face of Midnight bending over her eyes, his rough tongue licking her cheek, enjoying the salt and juices from her dying body. A butterfly danced just out of reach. Then she felt the sting of the green bottle fly on her lip, but it was no longer possible to brush it away.